Ahora imagina qu[...] pese a la vida de rec[...] [...]os de otros, Dios confía en ti y te llama a confiar en El y a mostrar valentía y compasión hacia otros con la finalidad de llevar a cabo su plan.

Éste es el caso de Rajab, quien a riesgo de perder su vida, decide ayudar a los espías y los esconde cuando toda la ciudad de Jericó se encuentra en su búsqueda, y posteriormente los ayuda a escapar. En su interacción con ellos es evidente que detrás de todo ese dolor, abuso y desprecio al que se había visto sometida y en el momento de mayor desafío, se revela un gran corazón lleno de bondad hacia alguien en necesidad, amor por su familia y confianza en el cumplimiento de la promesa por parte de Dios:

"Por lo tanto, les pido ahora mismo que juren en el nombre del Señor que serán bondadosos con mi familia, como yo lo he sido con ustedes. Quiero que me den como garantía una señal de que perdonarán la vida de mis padres, de mis hermanos y de todos los que vienen con ellos. ¡Juren que nos salvarán de la muerte"

Josué 2:12-13

Los espías escapan, Josué prepara la conquista de Jericó y los Israelitas toman posesión de la ciudad, en medio de todo el caos y la inminente destrucción sucede lo impensable y los únicos en salir con vida fueron Rajab y su familia:

"Ahora bien, Josué les había dicho a los dos exploradores: «Vayan a casa de la prostituta, y tráiganla junto con sus parientes, tal como se lo juraron.» Así que los jóvenes exploradores entraron y sacaron a Rajab junto con sus padres y hermanos, y todas sus pertenencias, y llevaron a toda la familia a un lugar seguro, fuera del campamento israelita. Sólo entonces los israelitas incendiaron la ciudad con todo lo que había en ella, menos los objetos de plata, de oro, de bronce y de hierro, los cuales depositaron en el tesoro de la casa del Señor. Así, Josué salvó a la prostituta Rajab, a toda su familia y todas sus posesiones, por haber escondido a los mensajeros que él había enviado a Jericó. Y desde entonces, Rajab y su familia viven con el pueblo de Israel".

Josué 6:22-25

La mujer indecente, de quien menos se hubiera esperado algo y mucho menos ser un instrumento dentro del plan de Dios; fue parte fundamental. La Biblia la menciona en el cuadro de honor de la fe (Hebreos 11:31) y lo más admirable es ver cómo una decisión de fe le hizo ser parte de la línea ascendente de nuestro Señor y Salvador Jesucristo:

"Salmón, padre de Booz, cuya madre fue Rajab; Booz, padre de Obed, cuya madre fue Ruth; Obed, padre de Isaí; e Isaí, padre del rey David. David fue el padre de Salomón, cuya madre había sido la esposa de Urías;...Así que hubo en total catorce generaciones desde Abraham hasta David, catorce desde David hasta la deportación a Babilonia, y catorce desde la deportación hasta el Cristo».

Mateo 1:5-6,17

Una muestra clara y contundente del poder renovador de Dios, de su compasión y que no hace excepción de personas.

Muchos de nosotros caminamos por la vida llenos de dolor, desconfianza, amargura y resentimiento. Inclusive dentro de la Iglesia podemos llegar a sentirnos indignos a pesar de haber sido perdonados. En ocasiones es inevitable que el peso de nuestros errores y pecados nos hagan sentir que no valemos la pena y que jamás seremos capaces de recibir y ver cumplir las promesas que Dios tiene para nuestras vidas.

Lemons:

In an Orchard

Lemons:

In an Orchard

David John Baer McNicholas

ghostofamerica ltd co

Copyright © 2022 ghostofamerica ltd co All
rights reserved
The characters and events portrayed in this
book are fictitious. Any similarity to real
persons, living or dead, is coincidental and not
intended by the author.
No part of this book may be reproduced, or
stored in a retrieval system, or transmitted in
any form or by any means, electronic,
mechanical, photocopying, recording, or
otherwise, without express written permission
of the publisher.

ghostofamerica ltd co
10401 Montgomery Pkwy NE STE 1A,
Albuquerque, New Mexico, 87111
ghostofamerica.net

ISBN-13: 979-8-9854752-1-0
Cover artwork by: Marla Allison
(marlaallison.com)
Library of Congress Control Number:
2021925568
Printed in the United States of America

DEDICATION

For You, may you find your own river.

Table of Contents

ACKNOWLEDGMENTS

Thanks to my first readers: Marla Allison, David Hagerty, Nathan Ritzo, and Christy Georg.

A novel is just a manuscript without a cover. I found my cover in the mind/heart/work of Marla Allison. marlaallison.com It is only through her sorcery that this manuscript is now a novel. Thank you Marla.

Lemons:

In an Orchard

REPORT

In September of 2020, human remains were discovered on an unnamed industrial farm in Southern California. The following account was retrieved from a handwritten journal discovered among those human remains. The corpse was severely mauled by wild animals. Though the body was identified through dental records, due to the intimate personal nature of this account, we have withheld the identity of the victim, out of good taste and an abundance of preemptive shields against litigation by the estate.

1— NO STUPID HATS

can't see my face. I'm sure I look rough. I feel around my cheeks, the back of my skull is sore.
There must be a few bruises there. A little dried blood crumbles off my forehead into the palm of my right hand. A semi hard and wet spot at the back of my skull stamps a bloody print onto the probing fingers of my left hand. I pull down the waistband of the jogging pants and inspect an injection site. They really jammed it in there in a hurry. It was a muscular injection, but it did the trick all right. There is a bruise the size of a grapefruit where it went in. My jacket is gone entirely. From what I can see of myself, I look like I've been rolling around in the dirt.

Lemons: In an Orchard

There is a contusion on my left elbow and right knee. My back feels like I slept on a pile of rocks. This is likely a reality, since that's more or less where I woke up. A strange small circle of stones under a lemon tree. A makeshift witch's rite of protection, though in this case I'm pretty sure protection wasn't on the minds of my abductors. They didn't grab me up and throw me out here in a ring of rocks to protect me from some imminent threat to my well being. More the other way around. This is a message. Whether the message kills me or not is yet to be seen. It's not totally hopeless. I have no water, but I'm in good shape for my age. One of the benefits of success like mine is a more than rudimentary amount of free time to stay fit.

The first animals I notice are bees. There aren't many flowers left. There's only one type of plant out here, lemon tree, and they've all gone to fruit. So the bees are just kind of here. It's too early for them to hibernate. How far could they travel to keep busy before they might as well move? They are small. Honeybees with transparent wings and fuzzy abdomens. They cling to the fruits and scan their little bee horizons for infrared signals that I feel pretty certain aren't out there. At least they aren't hornets. One lands on my leg. I brush it off quickly, startled. I don't like bees. They say they're all dying, and whoa, what are we gonna do? I'm gonna sip a margarita in my backyard without looking in it first to see if there be any stranded drowning little idiots with tiny nuclear warheads on their asses.

Insects like this will also feed on corpses. They don't talk about it much, but these guys will eat pretty much anything. Maybe that's how hornets came into existence. A hive of honeybees got the taste for flesh from chewing on a decomposing rabbit and the next time something chewed it's way out of a hexagonal incubation chamber it was this bloodthirsty crazed war machine that ate up its whole family before running out of the hive and amok among the flowers in the field, which it could probably still see with honeybee clarity but now was only enraged by.

It's too late bees. Go home.

At least my legs aren't broken. I stumble a little, the first signs of exhaustion and dehydration appearing around mid afternoon. The gold Movado on my wrist tells me so, of course it could be lying. The fact that I still have a six hundred dollar watch on tells me something about the reason I'm out here. It has nothing to do with simple robbery. My feet are sore. My neck is pounding and red from where I haven't been able to keep the sun off it. The smoke in the skies blots out the yellow orb which I know to be tracking my every move. The shadow which forms weakly to the front right works its way to the rear, at which point my forehead will feel baked and blistered unless I find some way to make a hat out of lemon branches. Now there's an idea. I refuse to wear a stupid hat though, and my resolve to be rescued is strong enough where I'm willing to forego looking like a jungle refugee for the time being and accept a little sunburn

3

from this hazed out sky. I won't be out here more than a day. Someone will be looking for me. Plus, there's got to be some kind of traffic out here. It appears to be an active farm, at least the trees are pruned and the fruit is ripe.

I look up, where there is no specific sun, just a deluge of solar radiation seemingly coming from every direction, even up from the ground. Ash falls from the sky like it's trying to snow. There is a hawk flying overhead. At least I hope it's a hawk and not a vulture. He's circling, but not necessarily over me. Maybe there is a rabbit down here or something. He flies off to the left while I watch him. He dives into the foliage and disappears.

It's funny being blinded by the repetition of forms and colors and little else. So many greens, more than in a box of crayons. I start naming them to keep my mind from gnawing on itself. I start with leaf green then realize how stupid that sounds because they are all leaf green. Some of them are darker, like jade or malachite. so I've got jade green. Then some are lighter like the exo-skeleton of a praying mantis or lacewing. So then I've got lacewing green. Pretty soon I'm running out of direct comparisons. I begin with more distant connections. Sour green comes to me when I think about eating a lemon, though that really should have been a yellow. It was a yellow-green, but I've already decided that colors named after other colors really won't cut it in my custom crayon box of greens, grays, browns, and one monolithic sun-bright yellow standing out among the rest, solitary of wavelength, bringing all the attention to itself even as it

4

perches behind and under green awnings and facades of leaves. There is only one yellow.

I'm not a religious man. I don't believe in karma. Still, if I make it back from this, I know some people who are gonna be on my shit list. I think about revenge. What I'd do. I think that I probably wouldn't have enough patience to drop them in the middle of some expanse of ironically inedible fruit. Leave them for dead. I begin to think how I'd like to see them suffer, and then I wonder if there are cameras out here. Am I paranoid yet? I will be if I don't find my way out of here, I'll go mad.

I don't belong out here. I mean nobody does, it's not a livable place. Just miles of trees and the only fruit in sight, lemons. Yellow, like the sun would be if there weren't all this smoke drifting down from the fires up north. If I had had a choice in the matter I might have asked to be stuck up there. At least if I didn't choke to death on smoke, there would be a slight chance of rescue. There doesn't seem to be anyone around here at all. You'd think they'd be out here picking fruit. They look ripe to me, but so far I ain't seen a soul. Not that I really like other people that much, but they're kind of necessary unless you're a survivalist, and I don't know what's worse, dying of thirst or starvation in a lemon grove, or spending your entire life preparing to survive such a thing. I am well beyond the point of that being a choice, and if I survive, I intend this to be a one-off adventure.

This was just an accident. It's all a big mistake. It doesn't pay to try and do the right thing. These trees are my reminder of that. That, for all my brilliance, I couldn't see this coming. How I could be so far above everything, then get slammed right down into this god damned repeating maze. This must be what wage workers feel like.

First, I tried running. I thought, it can't be that far. So I just ran. These stupid sharp branches tore at me. I've just got a t-shirt on, and pants. I got out of breath pretty quick, and my throat super dry. A couple low slung fruits punched me in the face as I ducked under a branch. This knocked me right over. I sat there for a minute thinking again about my day so far. A rabbit bounded through my vision. It stopped and looked at me with that typical rabbit case of Parkinson's. His nose shivering in my general direction. I thought of ways to kill it. None of them soon enough, cause he ran away when I jerked my leg in frustration.

I am fucking thirsty. I haven't had a drop of water all day. The tranqs wore off around seven am, I started shivering a little bit. There was this feeling, kind of unbelievable, you know you get that feeling sometimes when you wake up after a bender, like this hollow sinking nakedness in your gut. It screams, you! have. fucked. up. the. last. time. Then if you're at home and you're anything like me, you'll find the quickest way to change that feeling possible. After a few minutes, it kinda wears thinner, and you remember how bad it was, but you start to feel like you were maybe over reacting. This time, there is nothing between me and this feeling. And it doesn't go anywhere. There is nothing to take it away. Just lemons.

I woke up with a dry mouth. Now it's some time after noon, I've recycled all my spit thinking about what it would be like to bite into one of these little yellow bastards. Every time I let my mind go and in my imagination my mouth tastes this, my salivary glands shoot off rounds like an underage boy in a brothel. That's fucking gross. Now I've got that thought about boy semen, but the simile places it in my mouth, which was unintentional and distasteful, more so than the original simile. And despite all this, my glands are now unable to produce any more spit, so they just convulse painfully instead.

So, I decide to eat a lemon. They are, after all, the only thing I could catch out here that is remotely edible. I'm thinking maybe I'll evolve on the spot, develop acid concentrating glands and leave here with full acid pouches, go and find those sons of bitches who fucked me and spit in their faces. Na, more likely I'll just puke, but I really gotta try. If I get out of here and I read about a guy who had the same experience as me, only he taught himself to eat lemons, got used to them, even craved them, and discovered that the lemon diet cures cancer and hemorrhoids and all sort of nasty shit, well, I'd feel like a sucker for sure for not trying.

I shouldn't have tried.

I pick a fresh one. It is flawless, heavy, like a sun-drop jewel. I toss it casually in the air and catch it, like one does in a park with a ball. I am warming up. I stop and hold it to my nose and sniff. It has all the qualities of concentrated sweet and sour, with a little bit of floral edge that usually turns to a detergent note by the time it gets to the shelf at the grocery store. I sink my fingernails in the rind just a little, hear a little pop, see a spray of atomized oils whiff out into the air. I lick it and feel my tongue go numb. That might be my first clue as to how this is going to go. But I open wide anyway, ready to discover for myself. I bite it like an apple, if an apple were an electrified bucket of horse piss. It always tastes so good when it's used to cut the fishiness of a fried platter, when it is cut itself by a cup of sugar in a glass of lemonade, or even pickled in brine and juice, the rind becomes an edible candy treat, great on salads.

God, after the first bite I really want to stop chewing, but I think, of course this is hard. Of course it hurts. But maybe on the other side of the pain, sustenance. So I chew and the acid quickly finds every crack in my enamel, every nick on the inside of my mouth, my lips are numb and burning at the same time and the nerve response is like chewing on tacks without slowing down. My face curls up, my neck throws my skull into convulsions as the intensity grows with every bite. I am crying but I don't feel it.

The seeds and the skin taste the best. I wonder what this experience has done to the balance of moisture in my system as I greedily swallow back all the saliva it brings out. When I am done, I feel the charge moving down into my empty stomach. At that point I put two and two together and realize my stomach is about to dump more acid onto this acid bomb. Oops. I guess I should have known, but I was desperate. I double over. I heave. I heave as though dragging something out of my toenails through my spine and out my tongue. Yellow yellow bile and fruit remains spill out onto the brown dirt.

A drone flies overhead. It is carrying a lemon, likely for inspection. Running a program. A robot farm. But surely the drones don't do all the picking. I wave, trying to get its attention. When it seems to be unresponsive, I pick up a lemon and give it my best college baseball strike pitch. I nail the fucking thing and the effect is that it stops, turns and looks at me, as if to say, don't do that again. Then it turns back around and flies away. I toss another lemon after it, but I've wasted my arm on the first throw. My shoulder hurts. I heard something pop.

It's impossible to stay here. My mind takes me back over the memories of the years. Makes all the sweet spots painful, and the painful spots are points I fill with rage at the way I've been treated by the universe. I used to be quite successful. It was all a cruel joke though. What was my crime? Wanting more, perhaps. They all want more though, more of me than there is to go around. I have to satisfy so many hungry and vacant hands. They consumed me. And when I couldn't, didn't have any more to give, they stuck me out here, as if knowing their secrets were the worst crime I could have committed. Knowing how hollow and hungry they are.

I'm pretty tough, I might make it out of here. I've got to find some water though. In what I take to be the early afternoon as made evident by my watch, I look under a tree. The space beneath looks rather well groomed and shaded. It's time for a rest, so in I crawl. Brown and yellow dirt filling the fabric of my knees with humus, sand, and clay. The palms of my hands pricked by an errant patch of burweed makes me shout, fuck! My bare arms are already laced up and down with red stripes from some of the tight squeezes between the lower branches.

The underside of the foliage is lighter colors, the solar rays more diffuse. The ground is hard with root structure, but I am thoroughly too exhausted to give a fuck. I lay on my back like a broken action figure, my arms popped off laying next to me, my elastic spine is exposed, the paint on my nose is chipped and reveals an injection molded white plastic filler. God, I wish I was dead. No, no fuck I wish I wasn't here. Could anywhere be worse? The knowledge that I don't know what my wife and kids are going through adds to the torment of my situation. Would they have fucked with my family? I can't believe I hadn't thought of it before now. The images of murdered tortured bodies bring me to such a climax of pain, I lose consciousness briefly.

In my dreams I am hunted. That's nothing new. Maybe on some deep psychic level a part of me always knew this is how it would end. I'm in a sinister house. There are secret stairways and vast impossible rooms, tunneling basement churches where the lights go out just as I'm set upon by zombies. Sand covered floors with ceilings sloping down into dark corners where I feel drawn to put my hands. Locked rooms lit from within, others populated by coffins and characters who talk about me like I'm not there. The attics where vistas of public library bathrooms sprawl below in another kind of endless grid of stress holding.

In this one I'm walking along a trail on the side of a mountain. The path goes fairly parallel with the elevation even as it winds its way around boulders and under outcroppings. The sky is iron. The grass is plastic. The air is chilled and blasting my cheeks raw. I look at my fingers, gone already, evaporated in some caustic pool. There is something following me. Something is very close and getting closer. It howls. They howl. A pack of gray wolves with my hands for front feet. They've got voices which grab hold of my core like teeth sunk into my belt. The harder I run the closer they get, inevitably they will catch up. But they catch us all eventually don't they? None can escape forever. And how could anyone honestly say they were ready to give it up, unless they were one of those poor bastards pummeled already by life, dead kids and wife, cancer, framed for murder and molestation, infamous as a piece of shit that no one feels sorry for. The object of affinity for haters everywhere, including god. Maybe that guy will be me if I hang on long enough.

My eyes are open. I'm staring up through this beautiful green foliage. There are concentrated sun-drops hanging among the branches. They turn to condemned men all pointing their dead fingers at me. Fuck. I wake up with a start as one of the wolves grabs my calf between his powerful jaws and rips me out of my hiding place inside a very shallow cave. His growl echoes in the flat air the way no other sound does in this grove and I hear it inside my skull as that sickening stomach feeling of dread and regret consumes my attention once the dream passes. Then I hear a sound like someone taking a piss.

Next to my hand, still got all the fingers I checked, there is a stream of water poking out of the surface of the root grabbed ground. I stick my lips to the dirt and suck what must be a snapped irrigation hose. The water tastes like PVC and onions, but I don't care. It's not strychnine. At this point, I don't think a skull and crossbones label would stop me from tasting anything clear and liquid.

I suck the hose until I puke. That's unfortunate, and the water stops right after. Was my body able to retain any of that hydration or did I just lose more than I gained? I'm not an athlete, a doctor, or even a yoga instructor. I have no idea if I am closer to death or salvation at this point. I just know that my mouth tastes like the inside of a week old pizza box and my vision is fuzzy. I can see well enough to scribble down these notes.

I can see well enough in my mind's eye the things that brought me here and the people I've left behind. Anything between arms reach and the sky is just a frustrating maze of repetitious branches and leaves, and lemons, and they are occasionally blurring together like some impressionist landscape. Even without direct sunlight the shimmering shiny leaves are mesmerizing.

I've been sitting in a pile of vomit, considering eating the wet dirt to suck the moisture back from the earth. The thought leads me to believe that would make me puke again, and probably harder, and lose even more fluid. I'll just have to be more conservative next time. The thought of me being more conservative wracks my body with a spasm something like a wounded giggle. Oh, if they could hear me.

Back home, if I were there, I'd be sitting down for an afternoon scotch before closing out my business for the day. I'd take another glance at the market. Send out another email telling so and so what to do when to whom. My work isn't very exciting. I work with a group. Angel investors, kinda. We take over struggling businesses showing otherwise potential for profit, and we make money. I don't indulge much. So, I'd finish my scotch and lock my study. After that I'd go for a run. The streets around my home are patrolled twenty four hours a day by a private security outfit, which is why it's so hard to believe I was kidnapped from my own neighborhood. Me, an adult male in the prime of my life, in fighting shape no less. It all happened so fast. That first hit to the head blinded me with pain and a bright flash. After that, I struggled. I think I felt a nose crush under my fist, heard a distant grunt as one of my knees came into contact with something big and soft. But it was too late, They got a rag over my mouth which muffled my shouting and tasted sweet and pungent. Then a stabbing pain in my leg and I'm out. Shit. I really didn't need to relive that right now. I was just trying to have a scotch and take a jog away from this madness, this isolation and fear.

I think the point is, I'm a conservative and a neo-liberal. Your kids call me a fascist, and I'm fine with that. I have more than enough resources to be content and comfortable upon my mountain of personal accomplishments. My net worth is upwards of eighty million dollars. Which is one of the frustrating things about my present situation. If those retards knew who they were kidnapping, if I had a chance to tell them. I could have bought my way out of this.

If they haven't been otherwise affected by this, my family must have reported me missing by now. I know we don't spend a lot of quality time together, but surely my absolute absence has been noticed. I'm under no illusion that I understand them. I don't know how to be loving. And I don't see a problem with that. I take care of them. That's how I show my feelings. I honestly don't think I have emotions the way other, lesser people do. Stoicism has always come naturally to me. There is nothing to be gained from sentimental wallowing. Maybe this discipline will account for my salvation out here in this maze that's all turns and no dead ends. I'm sure if I just keep walking in one direction that I'll find my way out of here.

You know something else that perplexes me? They took my jacket and my phone. They left my expensive dumb watch. And they stuck this empty journal in my pocket with two pens! In case I lost one or ran out I guess. They must have known I'd have a lot of thoughts come to me out here and in some last moment of compassion thought it would be helpful for me to be able to take notes. And my shoes, they left me my shoes. My runners are looking pretty ragged, this will probably be their last mission. The jogging pants I was wearing when I was abducted were appropriate for a jog around the block. They are sorely unequipped to deal with the qualities of this trail. Tears up and down the outside of the legs, my balls are soaking wet inside what amounts to a plastic bag. I'm both too hot and shivering cold at the same time. What I wouldn't give for some cotton trousers right now.

* * *

West, I'm going West. That's what the shadows tell me. I should be near the I-five, maybe, or the other one, shit. I can't remember. It doesn't matter. What I do remember is that one trip with Darby and the kids when they were little. I think Chet was about eight. That was the year we got divorced. That trip was hell. I still don't know what that woman wanted from me. I don't even know if she got what she wanted from me. We drove most of that trip trying to fight in secret in front of the kids. It never works, kids are like dogs, they pick up on everything. Not that we were good at subtle by that point.

I remember we were driving up the five, going to Malibu from San Diego. We took the kids to the zoo and Malibu was supposed to be a little something special for us adults. Not that the kids wouldn't enjoy it, but you know, we had a sitter planned through a friend and we were supposed to try and salvage what remained of our marriage, you know, for the kids sake.

Right in the front seat of the car she gave me this look. It was a look I'll never forget. Almost like we were friends again, and she was about to pull a real mean prank on me or something. But we weren't friends. All she said was, Daddy's gonna take you to the movies tonight. Soon as our bags were checked she disappeared. She came back the next day and took the kids with her. Got on an airplane and just went home. I drove back alone. I mean, I wasn't in a hurry. This was the family trip and if the family wasn't going to participate, I'd just go home. I tried to stop at some of the roadside attractions that we had planned on seeing, but it just didn't feel right. There was no reason for me to be there.

By the time I got home, she'd tried to pull some bullshit with that fucking Lyons. He's a snake, that's for sure. But, I have my own pet snake. And mine is a mammoth. Looks like a shrew, but he's a mammoth. Don't fuck with those little guys. That was the end of that. Not really, I mean it took about a year. The kids went through hell, but honestly I was relieved.

I got lucky after that. I found Lisa. She gets me. Which means she handles her own shit and lets me handle mine. There isn't any problem I have that I can't make worse by spreading it all around and stinking up everyone else's atmosphere. Fuck, Lisa. I hope you're okay. I hope nothing happened to you and the girls.

The sun is gone. I can't really see the paper anymore.

2— AN ECONOMIC EXCHANGE

After the sun went down last night, things got very bad.

I was sitting under a tree, when I heard a terrible noise. Coyotes sound a bit like a nursery on fire. There were a lot of them and they were close. I sat wondering for about five minutes if they knew I was there. The sounds got closer. I climbed the tree behind me. It was about thirty feet to the top. The branches could bear my weight about two thirds of the way up. My eyes had adjusted to the light, what little of it there was after the moonlight had filtered down through the haze of the smokescreen and clouds. I could see movement below me. Heard their excited yipping. Perhaps they thought they had me in a good spot. Perhaps they did. One by one they made attempts to climb to my location. They weren't terrible climbers, but they were not arboreal acrobats either. A few of them got close to me. I could smell their awful flesh. They came at me growling and looking tough. They must have been very hungry to try an aerial attack like that. I held on tight with my hands, kept one foot planted on the branch below me solid, and kicked at them brutally. I felt my foot through my shoe connecting with their bodies buried in fur and bristle. The sound they made when I connected was pitiable. The sound they made when they hit the ground from a twenty foot drop was even more painful to hear.

Kicking coyotes out of a tree was like giving job interviews in a way. The first couple were weak, younger and less experienced. I could see it in their tentative movements, their eyes looking every which way as if to continually gauge the depth of the shit they were in. Then there came an older dog. He moved more fluidly. The gaze of this animal was frightening. The others had been comic relief up until now, the opening acts. This one was the headliner. He moved silent and smooth through the tree. When he came nearly within striking distance, he stopped. Fixed his eyes on mine. There we stayed, perhaps communicating in a sense. Interviewing each other as to which one of us would be dinner. He let out a low growl and then howled arching his salted and peppered face high to the nonexistent moon. I had been still and silent, but I let off a shout at him. Not words, just a gorilla noise, as though I were drawing on the distant reserves of strength of simian ancestors. He took my challenge and leapt at me. I swung around to the other side of the trunk and he sailed past me and tried to land on an out-swept branch. I kicked at him and missed, as he stumbled off the end of the branch and disappeared silently into the black void beyond the end of the visible tree. After a few more attempts they stopped climbing and waited for me to come down. Eventually I passed out, my bulk wrapped around the trunk of the tree. My head nodding against a yearling branch.

Somewhere in the twilight mind between nodding off under threat of assault and waking up cold to a hazed out sunrise, a reminiscent mood overtook my thoughts. It's hard to measure time in a less than conscious state, but perhaps the images that flashed before my mind's eye came just before the break of dawn, in the silent void between night shift and day. I woke up with memories of a paper mill.

❋ ❋ ❋

I don't understand people individually. I think that on an individual level people don't make sense, they are emotional, unpredictable, erratic and generally that just makes me lose my patience. I am a rational person. I believe that everything has a cause and a solution. Groups of people make sense to me. The law of large numbers. Groups are predictable almost infallibly when you have the right data or intuition.

I was in charge of the total turnaround of a paper plant in Maine. The company I was with had gone in on the investment, but they were pretty disappointed getting into the nuts and bolts of the restructuring. It seemed to many of my company managers that we had invested in a hopeless mess that was about to implode in a final bankruptcy. Of course it was, of course we did. That is what we did. Only this mess was a little deeper than my colleagues were capable of seeing through without becoming hopelessly mired in details. So I volunteered to take it on as a personal project. I enjoy a challenge. So, I moved to Maine for the summer.

I rented a cottage in Lisbon and drove to Lewiston, where the mill was, every day of the week for six months. I think that in restructuring people often overlook the small changes in favor of the big ones. It was certainly important that we fire and replace the directorship which had driven the company so far into debt and unmanageability, but afterward, what then? I find that people need clear space to function correctly. They need to have the garbage taken out. I don't just mean the trash bags from the break room. That stuff is obvious. But, junk piles up in plain sight all the time, you just have to know where to look.

Lemons: In an Orchard

I went down to that mill on a Sunday, when no one else was working. They could have been working on Sunday, but the state of the company was so besieged that the payroll had to be cut back in order to float through the end of the previous year and no one had been able to make those hours reappear on anyone's schedule since. The place was a mess. I looked around at that dysfunctional wreck, sensing out the logical weak points of the system.

This was a big place. If you've never been in a Maine mill building, especially a paper mill, they're huge. Some six stories tall with twenty foot ceilings on the ground floor, twelve foot ceilings on the upper levels. It stretched for an entire block long and half a block wide, with a parking lot taking up the other half of the block. I went from room to room, methodically checking out the contents of each space. What were they using it for, how was it contributing to the function or the dysfunction of the whole. My methodology with people and businesses is centered on the use of space and the allocation of resources.

I found room after room filled with the dust of decades. The evidence of neglect was so thick I had trouble walking through it. Hundreds of thousands of cubic feet of space packed tight with defunct machinery that had been brought in for repair, or whole divisions shut down for maintenance, obsoleted before they could be fixed, held in stasis as if waiting for time to return to them. Paper files going back a hundred years filled cabinets lining wall after wall of office space. It was as if, when they filled an office with records, they'd just move their desks into the next room and start the process over again without ever purging. In the loading dock area, I found that four of the five loading bays had been shut down due to an accumulation of broken forklifts, skidsteers, and an agglomeration of picnic tables. Everywhere I touched, my fingertip came away smudged with the lampblack of the boilers mixed with the sedentary particles of idleness. There were thousands of windowpanes. They were all choked with this thick, barely translucent layer that looked like it had been applied by spray can overnight, but had accumulated slowly, imperceptibly. It was this kind of growth by neglect that I found in just about every business I salvaged. It made my flesh ripple with goosebumps to know how easy this would be.

On Monday I had a meeting. I'd had my assistants go through the employee review records, which were undoubtedly spotty, and I had my two lists. I gave out pink envelopes and yellow ones, so everyone knew where everyone else stood without having to go through any idle chitchat or banter. Save it for the pub, I said. Those of you who got the yellow envelopes, I said, you've been selected to be part of the restructuring. They all just looked at me. They were stunned and silent, but not from my firing half of them, that had been a long time coming. Their minds were suffocating from the same level of stasis and neglect that had so deformed their mill over the last hundred years. Comfort and stability afforded to the few at the top had allowed things to degrade from the bottom up with very little notice taken of it. To be a part of this system as it was was to be partially degraded. Those I had selected for salvage, seemed salvageable to me.

There was one kid, he wasn't that young, but he was respected, well liked and strong enough to change with the times. His name was David I think. I set him the task of removing every single piece of junk and garbage from the plant. He said, do you want to try and recoup any money from this stuff?

I said, don't waste any company time trying to sell any of this stuff. Get rid of it in the most efficient means possible. We can't have local contractors running all over the place breaking legs and suing the company. Just rent some dumpsters, and put everyone to work. If there is anything too big to handle, come to me and I'll see to it myself.

Uh, yes sir, He said.

It took six months. By the time we were done cleaning out the old and useless crap, all the people who had managed to stay with us through the process all felt invigorated and renewed. They could see the changes. They could feel them, and they were a part of the solution. All the place needed was a house cleaning. It started with the top, the entrenched lazy corporate level people feeding off the teat of the still somehow functioning company even as it floundered under their guidance, but it had to go all the way down to the mop boards and the floor tiles.

For my upper end of things, I researched modern methods of the industry. I learned to streamline the processes and cut the ones that weren't profitable altogether from the equation.

I gave everyone a job. If some employee appeared before me, lost and wandering because he'd arrived to find the division he'd pioneered in the nineteen seventies shuttered and locked or thrown headlong into a dumpster, I'd give the man a mop and tell him to clean something, anything, I don't care what. It took one hundred people over a month just to clean all the windows. I made that one man's entire life mission after that, to keep those panes transparent and shining like a light bulb.

I brought in new practices, new machinery, new investors, new clientele, all on my own. That's my particular charm. And when I walked away from that town in the fall, I can tell you they were in good shape and had been returned to a profitable position. What they've done with the place since, I can't say. It just takes a little vision to do what I do. A lot of the time that vision is just the ability to see through the scads of junk and wasteland ethics which permeate the folds of an organization down to its roots. Admittedly, you have to have a non-sentimental personality. You have to look at people both as parts, but also as a whole, an organism. I don't really care whose grandmother died this week and who needs the day off to care for their sick kid. What matters to me is that according to the sociology and the statistics, the people showing up to work are doing so with a clear head and clear direction.

It was the summer after that paper mill restructuring that my first wife left me. After she was gone, I threw out everything we had ever owned together, and most of the things I had accumulated before that. I can't have things sticking to me, dragging me down into this mire of unaccountable slack where I can't let go of a specific chair because so and so's grandfather made it in shop class. It's broken, and it was made in a shop class. It has no value and no use. Throw it out. After Darby left, the last thing I needed was something to remind me of the utter failure of that relationship. Her implacable disposition, the way she'd use the kids against me over something completely fucking inane. That bitch was troubled.

She took the kids of course. Even in the nineties, men's rights were pretty uncomplicated, as a father, you had no rights. It's not that different today really. It took me years to get to the point where Chet would even talk to me. Melissa, she was daddy's girl of course. It's different with daughters and fathers. Sons are another story. There is some inherent complication, some competition, and ultimately some form of mental and emotional poisoning of the boy against me by his mother. When it comes down to irreconcilable differences, I'm pretty sure some of the difficulty he and I have is genetic, or that she raised him fucked up and there isn't much I can do except try my best to reach him.

He got into some trouble as a young man. He was trying to copy me I think, only he went at it all wrong. Then he got frustrated, and as young men sometimes do, he lashed out at the woman he was dating. I bailed him out and calmed her down. She wasn't hurt, just scared. He hated me for interfering in that. Told me that he wasn't a child anymore that I had no right to come into his life now and start ruining things. I told him I had kept him out of jail, that he should be grateful, but that I understood why he felt the way he did, because his mother had him so confused about life. He just about hit me, which I could have taken. I trained him myself, so I know what he was capable of at that age, and while I wasn't scared for myself, I certainly wasn't comfortable with his demeanor around that young woman.

When they broke up he didn't understand why. He drank a lot for a while, then appeared to settle down. Started coaching basketball for kids. His temper was still bad, but being around the kids had a calming effect on him. I figured it was good for him to be around people who were essentially of his own maturity level. He didn't really seem to be doing anything with his life, but at least he was behaving, and maybe through the intervention of sport and being a mentor, he could arrive at some place of serenity with himself. Maybe he'd even be able to find a woman who would care for him and put up with the defects from his rearing which he would probably never overcome completely. Maybe. Last time I saw him he was pretending to be putting a business plan together. Just like dad I thought. Only I also knew, there would be no way in hell he'd pull it off. Something was missing in the boy.

* * *

I wake up with these memories fading and rub my forehead. There are familiar sounds below me. Conversation! Not in English. People! I am saved. I groggily croak out a hello from my perch above them. They are startled and scatter into neighboring trees, leaving behind a campsite beneath me. I stiffly climb down the branches one by one, being very careful not to fall. My limbs are on fire from the experience of sleeping in a tree. I talk out loud in supplicating tones. Don't be afraid, I need help. Ayuda? I ask. Por favor? I don't know much Spanish, but it seems to make an impact. One of them comes out from hiding and stands below the tree while I climb down gingerly. His face is suntanned and brown. His eyes are a bit native, small and dark. In my excitement I stumble on the last few branches, luckily they are close to the ground and I kind of just eat shit in the last couple feet, landing sprawled on all fours. My knees strike hard on the half buried root systems. I squelch a shout of pain, make an awful face instead. He looks like he wants to help, but it's obvious the damage is done in this moment and best for me to regain some dignity on my own. I'm not a child.

After I recover, I sit on the dirt and look at him. He's short, like five feet tall. He eyes me like a nervous dog. I say, what's your name?

Waldo, he says.

¿Dónde está Waldo? I ask.

Que? he says before the shadow of suspicion lifts from his face and he smiles then laughs quietly. Now that he looks less serious, I can see that he's only about twenty years old. He has a bloody scab over his left eye. The others are coming out of the next tree over and joining Waldo and I in a group discussion on how evil it is to grow millions of acres of nothing but lemons. I ask if they discovered the irrigation lines and it's news to them. They are digging up the lines and inspecting them within seconds. They ask, when do they come on? Several times a day I say, not knowing if that's true or not. I mean, they must, right? They look at my watch. I tell them they are going to lead me out of here, and I give the watch to Waldo. I've put him in charge. There is a lot more where this came from. Let me show you. Just get me home.

Truth is, I've bought and sold people like this by the thousands. You just gotta know how to work with them, what makes em tick. They all wanna do a good job, you just gotta clear the way for them. Remove obstacles to the streamlining of their work. They won't tell me what they are doing out here, which is as good as telling me they are illegal border crossers, probably lost on their way to a rendezvous. Or maybe, as I am hoping, they are following meticulous instructions on how to get through this grove.

The water hasn't come on yet. It's been an hour since we met. I have made a trade with Waldo. My watch for him to lead me with his group out of this checkerboard jungle. It is the only thing of value I had on me, but I promise to give them all a thousand bucks each when we get to civilization. I tell them I'm a doctor, and that I will treat them in my private practice. I promise them a safe place to stay in my town, if we can just get there. I pretend to check the pulses of each member of the party, giving them a thumbs up after each checkup. The children are amused. Maybe I went too far. Maybe I didn't need to make up such an elaborate cover story. I was out here checking the health of the migrant farm workers and got separated from the group by a thunderstorm. I lost my vehicle and my phone and even my proper clothes you know. It's hard to believe, but they don't understand most of it anyway. They seem to hear doctor and mas dinero.

It dawns on me how lonely this place is. Farms in storybooks were always places where people worked together, family style whether they were related or not. They are the sanctuary of the archetypes of honesty, simplicity, and labor values. This place is an industrial wasteland. I say to Waldo, should we go now?

Okay, he says.

You lead, I say.

Okay, he says. Then he speaks rapido to his clan and they pick up their asses and we move.

I'm watching Waldo as he leads us. Trying to decipher a pattern from his rights and lefts. He seems to know what he's doing, which could be confidence or con. If I was in better condition I could read him, but right now, I'm just glad he's not a coyote or a shapeshifter. Right, left, left, right. I lose track. I day dream a little in the wake of this quiet group. I think about a hooker I hired in Thailand. I look at the group, there are two younger women. They are dressed poorly, they haven't showered in a week, perhaps more. I try to imagine them with a bath and some makeup and decide they'd probably be alright in another setting. The human sex drive is incredible. Here I am fifteen minutes from death perhaps, in the arms of some Spanish speaking salvation army and I'm thinking about fucking a pair of them just to pass the time. Good thing Waldo can't read my mind. I'm probably checking out his sister. He's too busy trying to look like he knows where he's going anyway.

My watch shines unholy fire on his wrist. It dangles down around his palm. It's not one of my nice ones, just a Movado. They might be the only company in existence to fetishize Esperanto. What's six hundred bucks for a wristwatch? It's dependable and it looks good enough to wear to the gym. If I caught a squash ball across the bezel of a Rolex I'd be pissed about it, but this thing is cheap and indestructible.

Lemons: In an Orchard

They move quietly. Obviously they are practiced at not drawing attention to themselves. Me getting the drop on them from the top of a lemon tree is almost comical. I laugh, a chuckle. Waldo looks at me briefly, but he doesn't ask. It would be too much chatter. I watch the group. They are silent, but they communicate. They care for each other. There are seven of them. Two men, Waldo and Ignacio. Three women and two children. The women are all different generations. They could be related. The youngsters are vibrant but also quiet. They look at me more than the adults. A boy and a girl, but at their age, not a whole lot of difference. They both have brown eyes with that same native look to them. They are beautiful kids, but they have no business being dragged across international borders by what I can only surmise are irresponsible guardians.

The intimacy they express toward one another is unsettling. The women have smiled at their companions more in an hour than my wife and I have in a year. They touch each other and I see an old woman, obviously in pain, brighten and unfold. She is reinvigorated just by the steadying hand of the younger woman. They give each other strength. I think they are giving me strength. For a moment I feel like a thief. They have something between them which is both precious and foreign to me.

After a couple hours I say, let's check for water, no? Agua?

Agua, the word rises up through quiet murmuring to a dissipating chant. They look at the ground, tired and thirsty. Waldo and I crawl under a tree, they follow us and dig up the roots to find the hoses. They are dry, but we decide to wait and see. Siesta. We've walked all over hell today. It's been half the day and we haven't walked in a straight line for more distance than it took to arrive at a break between two trees. He keeps changing direction on us and honestly I get a little worried. I ask, Waldo, you sure you know where you're going?

Si, he says.

Bien, I say.

The water begins to flow out from the torn up tubing. There are three fountains running. They water first the children, then the women, starting with the oldest, Then they offer it to me. The men and I take a few gulps each before the pressure dies off and the fountains dry up. The elder woman comes over to me and says, doctor, por favor. She motions to the younger of the two other women. She makes a sign with her hand at her belly that says, this one is pregnant. Then she points at me and says, you check?

I don't know the first thing about obstetrics, but I know a thing or two about women. I put on my doctor face and approached the young woman. Of course she is pregnant. I kneel down and I say, how do you feel? She looks up at me and shakes her head, doesn't understand. I say, como esta? She says, ok. I say and motion, can I check your baby? She nods, ok. I lean in slowly, lift her shirt and put my hand on her belly. I close my eyes and wait to feel something. Her belly is just a little round, she's got some time to go before she'll be giving birth. I say, how long? When she shakes her head again, I ask Waldo, how many months?

Cuatro he says.

He speaks and she and I both feel a kick. We look at each other. She smiles reflexively. I smile back. I say, baby's fine, esta bien.

I see a very personal look of relief on Waldo's face. This is his baby. This is his woman I've got my non-doctor hand on. I pull her shirt back down over her swelling navel. I sit back on the dirt. my hand is shaking a little bit. Waldo sees it and asks, you okay?

Fine, I say.

He looks around at the group of tired huddled masses. Descansamos, says Waldo. We all recline in various postures under the tree. I hear him whisper one more thing, but I don't recognize the words. Esta fador, Dios lo está castigando. I fall asleep quickly, exhausted from the ordeal, unable to translate that last sentence.

3— STREAMS OF CONSCIOUSNESS

When I wake up, they are gone, and so is my watch. We've probably backtracked god knows how far and in what direction. I wasn't paying attention to the shadows, just following Waldo. I see now, that was a mistake. They were nervous from the start. They probably think I'm gonna turn them in as soon as we hit the pavement, which, maybe I would have. I mean, if they're gonna come into my country uninvited, the least they can do is be useful for a minute before we get them sorted. But, whatever. I don't need them. Nobody needs them, that's why they're out here. I'm not a racist. It doesn't matter to me where these people came from, if they are broke and have nothing going on in their lives at home, what makes them think that they will have anything more useful to do with themselves here in my country? My ancestors brought civilization with them. Yeah, they encountered some resistance, but where would we be if we hadn't? There is just no way that this country was going to remain untouched. If it hadn't been white Europeans it would have been someone else eventually.

I had another dream this afternoon while these illegals were abandoning me. I was arguing with my son. I told him to grow up. He did. Aged right before my eyes into a carbon copy of myself and continued to argue with me. That kid gets under my skin. I love him, but I wish he would actually grow up. Take some responsibility for himself. He doesn't have to be as successful as I am. It's not about that. I've made enough money for multiple lifetimes. He shouldn't even worry, just pick a path and find some peace in it. I don't know what his problem is honestly. I know that me and Darby split up, but that kind of thing happens all the time and people get over it. They move on. I'm just not sure that he ever will. Funny how much he looks like me. I can't get the image from the dream out of my head. It was like looking into a mirror while I aged in time lapse. How many parties, holidays, work days went by last night looking into his eyes while he called me selfish and cold?

I don't normally dream this much. Seems like the air, the exposure, or the overall stress of the situation is getting to me. I'm uncomfortable. I make a fist and let it go. I kick the dirt and scream. I grab one of the branches and twist it as hard as I can, thinking I'll break something and feel better. It resists. I lay on top of it thinking that with all my weight I will snap it off. I scream, fuck! and lemons topple from their perch into the dirt with a thumple thumple. I pick them up one by one and throw them as hard as I can. One explodes five feet in front of my face and the other one I throw so wildly that I skin my knuckles open on another branch. Lemon juice gets into the cuts and I curl up over my hand, a wince, a groan, and a growl.

The lines dug up by the group start spouting water. I plunge my torn knuckles under the stream and rinse the acid out of the wounds. I wish I had some sort of vessel to collect it in, but at the moment resign myself to drinking enough of it to quench my thirst, but not so much that I throw it back up. It is a minor relief, but it also means I won't pass out from dehydration and heat exhaustion quite so quickly. The flow stops. I'm sitting in a puddle looking and feeling like a toddler, or a confused monkey.

I see on the ground one of the men has left a jacket. They must have been in quite a hurry to get rid of me. I'm lucky they didn't slit my throat. That was really careless of me. Giving up my watch may have saved my life. I pick up the jacket. It's several sizes too small and it smells like another man has been wearing it without a shower for a month. I try to wash it in the mud from the exposed irrigation. It comes out looking about like you'd expect. Wringing it out, I sling it over my shoulder to dry. I look for the shadow. Without my watch I can't tell where it is supposed to be, but I know it's near the end of the day again. Another hour or two or walking in a straight line will get me somewhere as well as erase the taste of my failed coup of the group. I notice something else in the dirt. A pendant on a snapped chain. It appears to be gold. There is an icon inside a locket, opposite someone's mother. Aunts don't usually make it into these things. I pick it up and put it in my pocket, a souvenir, meaningless to me other than as a reminder of these other strangers who are out here in this grove wandering lost, now likely desperate to avoid running into me again as they've made it clear how they feel about me.

I walk in the direction I think is West. Vague shadow behind me and to the right. I walk along a row of trees, thirty feet tall and bushy. Branches nearly touching each other near the base, laden with yellow fruit and leathery shiny green leaves of every known and some unknown descriptions of the color. Verdigo, sea-sick, chartrueth, growing pains, life everlasting... The names become a stream of consciousness poem that I stop trying to understand. Envy, right of way, antifreeze. I walk on down the line. Most of the day has been wasted by those fools, and by this fool. It's getting dark, I'll put the pen away. But I'm going to keep walking until something stops me. I have lost some time today, but I feel a little more energetic than yesterday. Maybe that burst of anger was just what I needed to connect with my masculine vitality.

4— MY CURSED TEETH

I wake up in the top of another tree, shivering and not well rested.

The dogs came back last night. I managed to walk for a few hours in the dark. That is one advantage to there being such a clear path. I heard the yowling and yipping and climbed for shelter in the nearest tree top. They came on me quick and like the night before there was the one who was bigger and smarter than the others. He came up the branches like they were a set of stairs. When he was just below me he started snapping at my heels. I kicked down and landed a few good blows to his snout. Other dogs would have cried out. He didn't even flinch. I have a scratch on my leg where his teeth trailing along my pant-leg after a vicious kick had cut me as he tried a little too late to sink them into my flesh. The scratch itches like crazy and it's bright pink flesh looks infected for sure. If I was a doctor, I'd be prescribing some antibiotics and lots of water. After he realized he was gonna keep taking hits to the face unless he got out from under me he climbed to a long thick branch directly across from my position and at my level. Once again I parried with him around the tree trunk, and once again he disappeared silently off the end of a branch after a failed take down strike.

They circled below me, howling and making this awful strangled yelling sound while I hung tight, vigilantly focused on any other attacks they might attempt. A smaller dog came up the same way as the big one. He was quick and limber, but he was careless and weak and I landed a jab kick into his ribs. He cried and fell sideways and upside-down off the branch and landed with a small crash and a pitiable cry.

In my fevered dreams last night as I drifted in and out of a consciousness riddled with a type of mortal awareness, I found myself among a group drifting on an open sea. The sway of the vessel on the swell of the ocean. A vast undulating plain at night. The moonlight shattering into a trillion fractal shards. A dewdrop in a dewdrop in a dewdrop. I was the captain. I held the wheel in my grip, felt a pull and a tug. My men worked like ants. The creaking of the boards, the smell of salt and fish and a basket of limes, their flesh marked with brown spots from age. There was a sense of unrest. We drifted for days with nowhere to land.

Lemons: In an Orchard

Days turned into months. My sense of time dilated, though I kept making new notches in the mast every sunrise, another one always erased itself before I got to it. We were going to a place where it was warm and there was plenty of rum and casual sex with women. God knows how many of my crew were down below decks in furtive imaginative moments dressing up in straw skirts and coconut brassieres, lubing up each other's parts with chicken grease.

The months turned into years though and I could see my beard turning gray as I turned it over in my sun browned salty fingers. There were bees that lived in my beard and they drank the nectar from the flowers that grew in the crows nest and came back down and made honeycomb inside my head. Eventually they grew stronger than the crew. They developed a taste for meat and evolved into hornets driving the crew into the sea in lifeboats made of lemon rinds which quickly sank. The ocean was acid and dissolved their bones.

The bees and I sailed on for several lifetimes and still, there were no more islands, no more continents. It was as if the ocean had swallowed up all the land. I looked at the tattoos on my arms and chest and saw a story unfolding along biblical lines. Ancient knowledge, locked in libraries buried beneath a one world ocean, brought to life in my flesh. I knew that every book ever written or ever to be written could be found encoded in my DNA.

My Cursed Teeth

It was always night and the moon was always full. I would sit above the deck, twisted in the rigging as the hornets flew in and out of me without stinging. I pulled my ensnared arms and legs this way and that to adjust the sails like a little puppet controlling its master. The ship became an extension of my body and we drank the ocean. Whales beached themselves on the massive deck, which grew over the centuries as if it were alive or expanding with the universe so that the massive creatures jumping aboard barely made a sound and the deck boards barely flexed under their gargantuan weight. They were torn apart by the hornets who delivered their flesh to my tongue in my open mouth, my head now made of hexagonal chambers filled with squirming larvae.

One night, the only night since we started this journey a million aeons ago, while I gazed upon yet another gorgeous full bellied full blooded moon, a wave much bigger than the biggest. A wave so tall that it brushed the bottom of the lunar surface, wetting it, leaving the big blue cookie looking half dipped in milk, the milk of galaxies. This wave, so large and so slow but also so sudden, became the biggest thing in my world. My ship had grown to the size of a continent, but it was dwarfed by this wave that stood before me, so powerful it refused to break and held itself together on the force of the will of its size. How many water molecules? How many gallons seemed irrelevant, it would always take more. I knew it would continue to grow, no matter how long I watched it would never fall, but at the same time it

Lemons: In an Orchard

was always overtaking me, crushing me, drowning me. I became like dust, amoeba, diatomic plankton and I dispersed throughout the entire ocean. I dove with my eyeless sight down to the ancient cities from a billion years ago and entered the turnstiles of defunct subway stations where the skeletons of poor people had been reduced to calcium and nitrogen and swirled together in the spiral shells of giant mollusks which traversed the rotted rail tunnels like big stony rats. I saw the dead traffic lights, airfields scattered with aluminum air-frame skeletons, skinned by the chewing lips of parrot-fish. Repopulated with brain coral and branches of sponge throbbing in the dark well of cold and salt and thoughtlessness.

I became bio-luminescent and formed trails around where the new ocean currents met and the turbulent flow of evolution mastered nothing and tried all. Sparks from me found their way back and up into that massive wave standing now in my glow like a lighthouse. And the hornets came and ate my brains.

* * *

I awake from this dream, shivering and with beads of sweat on my forehead. The sun has just breached the horizon, and for a minute I think it's another wave, come to swallow me up. I climb down from this one same damn tree. At the bottom, sitting in a wicker high back with an inverted compound bucket to prop his feet, is an old man. He doesn't seem to notice me, so I say, hello.

He turns his head, gazes slowly in my direction. Are you a spirit? he asks.

I don't think so, I say.

He grunts. Not a spirit, he says. Did you see the eagle this morning?

I say, I think I saw a hawk two mornings ago.

No, he says, this morning.

When?

Just before you came down. I thought you were part of the same sign.

Sorry to disappoint you.

Disappointed people have no curiosity. The mice will eat their shoes. They have no heart.

I swear that's what he says to me. I kinda just look at him. He doesn't appear to be waiting for an answer. I ask him, what are you doing out here? This seems like an unlikely place for...

He cuts me off, an unlikely place, he says, copying my words. Did you see the eagle just a few minutes ago? Now he repeats himself. I have a feeling that the conversation isn't going anywhere until he removes his feet from the bucket, slides it off from a package beneath it and produces a luncheon wrapped in butcher's paper and twine and a small table with slender wire legs that just fits inside the bucket.

You're full of surprises, I say.

Sur-pri-zez, he repeats. The mice will eat your shoes man.

Not if I don't take them off, I say.

He grunts again as if, everyone says that. Are you hungry? he asks.

I'm starving actually, I say. And I mean it. I haven't eaten since I've been out here. I can only assume that I ate about three days ago, if my former watch was correct. I'd been unconscious during the abduction for about twelve hours. My stomach hurts. My head is buzzing. I walk with the rhythm of a zombie. It is uncomfortable, but I know as long as I don't lose consciousness and get cooked to death in the sun, I can survive roughly two weeks without food and that water, which had been graciously provided for me by this robotic farm, would be my primary resource without which I would not last two days.

Have some food then, he says.

Thanks, I say and I sit in the dirt opposite him at his ridiculous looking picnic table with its three wire legs. I must be wondering aloud because I say, why aren't they out here picking the fruit?

Pandemic, says the old man. As if he had been making sense this whole time.

Oh, yeah, I say, I kinda forgot about the pandemic. They won't let this fruit just rot out here will they?

How should I know, he says. His eyes bore into mine through cloudy blue irises. If the robot makes it, let the robot eat it. He veers back into oblique statements. Well, a half lucid old man with food is better than a maniac with a knife. He unties the twine carefully, his arthritic knuckles curved into talons picking at the knot which is not tied like a shoelace but like a pile of half-itches all pulled tight into a ball.

I say, would you like some help?

He says, mice will eat your shoes and points a crooked rheumatic wand in my face over the parcel.

Fine, I say, mice will eat my shoes. I watch him try to tickle the knot undone. He gives up on subtlety and his face doesn't betray any frustration as he slips his wrinkled thumbs under the twine, makes two fists and pulls hard. The twine both snaps and cuts into the gnarled skin of his hands. He doesn't make any sound to indicate his injury.

Yes, he says as he unwraps the bundle. Sitting atop the table are three sandwiches looking like they were made in an expensive deli, Each one cut into four triangles and pinned together with a flagged toothpick.

Flagged toothpicks always make me think of my uncle Milton. He told me this story of being at an airport restaurant in the nineteen eighties. This is back when air travel was still a cool thing to do and not an oppressive necessity. It was all a lot looser and more natural. Buy a ticket like you were hopping on a bus. It wasn't as stressful an event as it is today. He sat down and the waiter came over. What's good here? he asked.

The club sandwich is very popular, said the waiter.

Uncle Milton thought for a moment, do I like club sandwiches? I think I do, and he said, sounds good, bacon and turkey?

Bacon and turkey on sourdough, said the waiter. This is back before sourdough had made its big comeback with the micro-bakeries and the resurgence of microbial food stuffs in general, so sourdough was kind of an interesting touch. Milton became more interested by the moment. Of course, he had sat down about half an hour before his flight, and how long can it take to make a sandwich. He was very hungry, so whether it really took twenty minutes or not is up to interpretation. Regardless of the functions of the universe around him and this sandwich and this waiter at the time of the event, the event that took place is undeniably visceral and certain. When that sandwich came out of the kitchen, and Milton eyed the waiter nervously, probably saying to himself, my god man, it's not like I ordered a Monte Cristo for Christ's sake, in perfect nineteen eighties secular heresy.

No sooner than he had put the plate down did Milton's face relax. Milton thanked him and grabbed a quartered piece of this salivation inducing wedge of flavor and slipped more than half of it past his teeth into his mouth to chomp down, not only into the layers of meat and cheese and vegetable stacked between three pieces of bread, but for the sandwich to bite him back. Apparently those little flags are not ornamental. The toothpicks in Milton's sandwich did not bear any identifying insignia, and you could argue that his wanton carelessness is proof of the disintegration of western society. But, you would lack compassion and jurisprudence. Very few other people I know, have pierced their palate. It's actually kind of difficult, mostly because of the amount of nerves there. It's not super solid, but generally the amount of pain it causes is enough warning for a reflective person to back off. Milton was a reflective person by nature, but he was distracted by the pressure of the moment. Starving in an airport lounge with five minutes to eat a ten minute sandwich, and the bastard waiter hadn't even brought him a water to rinse this thing down with.

  I can only speculate as to the amount of pain he was in. When he was describing it to me, his eyes teared up and turned red. He said that more blood gushed from that wound than he had ever seen come out of his own body. Did he make the flight? Of course he did, this was the early nineteen eighties, before that stupid bitch sued Dunkin Donuts over hot coffee and the world was still largely made up of natural men and women, not this fucking crowd of risk averse analysts self cataloging every little cut and scrape they get in some hierarchy of value against a flow chart of dystopian insurance regime. He put down the sandwich, didn't even ask for his money back. Motioned for the waiter to bring him extra paper towels and a to go clam-shell. And when he got on that plane with a mouth full of napkins soaked in crimson human liqueur, the check-in attendant told him he couldn't bring his sandwich on board. Without a second thought he tossed the thing in the garbage can at the gate before getting on the plane to fly 3000 miles across the country where at the other side he presumably sought minor medical attention.

The sandwiches which sat on the table in front of me had flags on their toothpicks, and honestly I noticed, because ever since Milton told me that story I have made sure to note the position of every leave-in place kitchen implement on my plate. I once was feeding a girlfriend with a fork. I made the mistake of holding the fork wrong. It was perpendicular to the line of the lips instead of a flat parallel. She bit down as though she were going to take the end of the fork off, her teeth making this awful scraping sound which I can only imagine was a hundred times worse inside her head. She screamed and hit me. I felt bad, but honestly, you'd have to be stupid or unobservant to have bit down that hard to begin with. I never trust other people that blindly, especially when they are putting things near my face.

The old man hands me a slice of this magnificent sandwich. I hold it aloft like a toast and say, to the mice who will eat my shoes. He looks at me like I had just said the dumbest thing he's ever heard and picks up his piece and bites into it. I notice his teeth are in good shape for an old man, a little brown stained but solid. The sandwich tastes exactly like it should. Exactly like it looks. Strange thing is that it doesn't smell the same as it tastes. Maybe it isn't the sandwich. Maybe there is a corpse nearby under a tree that is wafting in my direction. Maybe it's my own body odor.

He shares half of each sandwich with me and we eat mostly in silence. He watches me strangely though. A couple times I have to ask him, is everything alright? He just looks as though he has been contemplating a spiderweb or some insignificant but intricate pattern and then loosens his gaze back down into his sandwich. When we are done there are a jumbled pile of twelve flagged toothpicks with green cellophane shredded and wrapped in tatters around the tops of the sticks.

He reaches into a satchel beside his chair and pulls out what looks at first like a spyglass. I wonder if he will be navigating. He holds it to his eye and squints the other one shut tight, folds of a thousand year old face just keep disappearing into his eye socket. I wonder when it will stop. Will his whole head get sucked in there and pop he just subsumes himself into the spyglass? The compressing wrinkles stop. That eye is for sure shut now. Then he takes his free hand and turns the front end of the barrel as though bringing something into focus. I can hear little shards and trinkets rolling around inside the tube. Then I realize the end facing me is full of multi-colored panels. The old geezer is blissfully occupied by a kaleidoscope.

Lemons: In an Orchard

He says, you've got a lot of blood on your face. At first I don't quite hear him. His words pass through me. Then I stop licking my lips and slowly reach up to touch my face. My cheeks are moist and slick. My fingertips play around on them in absent minded circles, sliding in spirals over the bones beneath my flesh. When I pull my hand down and look into it I see a dark brown patina obscuring my own flesh.

What is this? I ask. Thinking for sure that there was some explanation other than the obvious and horrible.

Mice are gonna eat your shoes, he says again, dropping the phony guru accent and sliding into a more colloquial tone.

I say, motherfucker, what the fuck did you do to me?

I'm not sure what you mean, he says. I shared what I had with you. He stands up while I am still stunned from the reveal that what I had seen as too perfect sandwiches is in fact the corpse of a dead dog, perhaps the one I had kicked from the branch the night before. The smell envelopes me. If you've ever smelt dog blood, it smells like the dumpster behind a butcher shop. It is inside my face, all over my hands and chest. There is fur lodged in between my front teeth. It tickles the backs of my lips.

He walks behind the tree, taking his bucket and table with him. The wicker throne becomes a climbing rose planted in memorial of some field hand or farmer's dead child. I can't find him after that. I can't recall his features other than that receding eyeball and kaleidoscope. If he even had a face in the fevered waking dream space of that repugnant meal.

I must have swallowed a good amount of flesh. I stand up, then I retch hard. The writhing dog meat kicks hard at the back of my chest. It feels like a colony of mealworms rolling around in my stomach, twisting and wriggling and gnawing at me. I've trained for thirty years in full contact martial sports of many different lineages. I can take a punch to the gut. This is not something I had ever trained for. My body has taken over and my mind is in revolt. I try to tell myself that people in other cultures have done this for millennia and that I am biologically no different than they are. It doesn't work. The smell of rotting hamburger mixes with the metallic tang of my own heaved up bile to create a cement of inescapable mental quagmire. I remember throwing up two days ago when I had found the water.

I look down and see water seeping up through the roots and soil below me and know it will be another four hours before the irrigation would spring again. I drop to my knees in my own pile of slippery puke and coyote entrails and spread the mess apart with my hands, like some psychopath cave painter filling in a bloody horizon acid etched into a limestone wall. I tear the dirt away feeling for strands of tubing. My fingertips catch on super light gauge PVC pipe. The black tubes I wrench loose from the soil and bite into them with my cursed teeth,

Lemons: In an Orchard

feeling the gush of clear true life splash into the back of my throat once before the system goes limp in my grasp.

5— INTESTINAL DISCOMFORT

I look up into the tree above and around me.

On my knees with my palms to the sky I hold across my lap a deflated moment of salvation. My being is streaked over in blood and guts. My body and mind fail to stay intact during this intercourse with fate. surely I am being pegged to death by some vengeful goddess who will not stop flagellating my helpless skeleton until I am once again the dust of the earth, and my pain and misery will water future life, insinuating the thread of decay itself which brings us all down eventually in this heartless universe. My concentrated arc of vileness running foul through every future generation as though I were some implacable dart, tearing out the hearts of generations to come by the frigid strength of my ceaseless hunger.

I grab several lemons from the tree above me and break them with my bare fingers into pulp and juice which I smear over my face and closed eyelids. I hold them above my open mouth and sorely drink of the sour running juices, gagging. I cleanse my teeth with the bitter foamy pith and leather yellow skin. I tear my blood clot covered shirt from my chest and throw it to the muck. Using the juice of several more lemons I cleanse the filth from my chest and arms. When I am finished, I put on the jacket from the immigrant sons of bitches who'd abandoned me and stolen my watch. My pants can't be helped, they were a frail mess layered with stink and blood and radical acid mixtures from my stomach and the growth from the tree above me.

I survey the murderous scene before me. The juice dried and cracked on my bare skin. Every movement I make reminds me how terribly alone I am, and have always been. I kick with my shoe at the corpse of the dog. Mauled and brutalized, it could be identified, but just barely, and not by anyone who was a stranger to this sort of charnel scene. I half expect it to bark or whine like it had the night before. I half wish it was still alive and that it would rise up and eat me from the bowels up. Like I had just done to it. We'd be a pair of zombies roaming with a ceaseless hunger through the endless graph paper maze of lemon trees, turning all the other coyotes into zombie dogs. They will all obey my command and soon we will find the escape from this repeating hell hole, we'll spill out into the real world again with an unquenchable thirst for vengeance on all them that turned their backs on us, left us out here to starve. Was I part coyote now? Would I turn with the full moon into a slightly more ravenous creature than I was before? There was a hollowness inside my gut I had little to compare with.

The gray smoke clouds roll inseparable from each other overhead. The sun disperses into ether when it hits that wall, becomes a hot plasma I walk through. Becomes part of the endlessness of the place, there are no rays, just heat and brightness, turnt up. The muddy jacket from the day before stretches across my shoulders. It is bedazzled denim and will not close in the front. There are about six inches of flesh between the buttons and the holes and no way conceivable to make ends meet. The light which had previously burned my neck and arms now comes back for my belly which protrudes from the clown clothes and leads the way into the scorched grove among the moving trees where the breezes do not stir. So it must be animals watching me, birds overhead. I look up, to see if there's another sign. I don't know what signs mean. Is it written in English? Is it laid out like a technical manual? Just don't tell me to feel for it, that's garbage. Everything has an explicit side. The universe is a causal map where one thing leads to another. That's how I got here and that's how I'm gonna get out.

Lemons: In an Orchard

I trudge on through the dusty dirt trying to time my next drink. Counting the trees go by, I have to start over about seventeen times and get completely flummoxed about how many that makes. I will escape from this prison. I have water, I can kill another coyote with my bare hands if need be and I'll eat him raw too and this time his flesh will stay down. I'll digest his fresh warm blood. I pull up the leg of my running pants and am dumbstruck by the amount of pain I am not feeling from the scratched leg which is now bulbous and wrong looking. Not sure how I am walking on it. So much like an oozing pink puppet, inflated into my shoe. Maybe it needs some air I think, so I pull the pant leg up further and fold it into itself to stay put, but it is a slippery nylon so it just falls back down and I say to myself, maybe not. Maybe sun is bad for it. Well, it doesn't hurt anyway, maybe it's healing. I look up in the sky again. This time there are birds. They are big. They fly in a big circle overhead. God damn it, who told you? I shout at the sky. Was it the rabbits? God damn the rabbits. I should have them all killed.

With supernatural sensitivity I hear the irrigation system booting up. It sounds like a million men taking a piss underground. It sounds like the beating circulatory system of a titan. Somewhere, there has to be a diesel engine powering this pump. I run for the cover of the branches and tear at the dirt. The soil is packed harder than the last and two of my fingernails bend backwards and snap off. I dig with the prints of my fingertips until I hit the muddy layer and rifle through the silt to find a hose which dries up as soon as I tear into it. I lick the ground where the water flows into the roots. My teeth are filled with dirt and when I move my jaw the sensation of silica crystal grinding between my teeth sounds like hard beans going through a coffee grinder. I look at my torn fingertips and lick the dirt and blood from them repeatedly until the blood stops.

I decide to wait here with the exposed water source for another watering. It seems to happen about every two hours or so. Can't really tell without my watch, fucking thieving Mexicans. If they've already made it out of this I hope they choke on a rat meat taco. This, this is murder what they did to me. Murder for the second time. It is mid morning when I sit down underneath this same lemon tree yet again, worse for wear. I pass out from weakness which overtakes me without warning.

* * *

I was playing in the street. Dad came downstairs and out the front door. He looked at me and I stopped playing. I said, dad do you want to play?

He said, playing's for babies. Are you a baby?

I said, no, dad.

I think you've got some explaining to do young man.

Lemons: In an Orchard

What do you mean dad?

Look at your room! He bellowed. His words like a spell transported us to a room I recognized. It wasn't my room, not quite. There was blood everywhere. My mother and sisters with their throats cut lay strewn about the room like dolls. My ex-wife and children and my Lisa, they were all bled dry and flopped in unnatural positions as though furniture were just boulders they had stumbled into while shaving with open straight razors.

I turned to my father, but everything went black. There was no light and I felt the ceiling pushing down upon me. I tried to get away, but the further I walked the lower the ceiling got. Even when I turned around I felt this crushing confinement.

I wake up under the tree screaming. Its branches laugh at me in the breeze that has struck up while I lay fitful and unrested below. My fingers and my leg are throbbing. So much for no pain. A trio of squirrels play a game of tag among the branches overhead. A lemon drops from a branch and hits the ground near me with a thwump.

I pick it up and bite a hole in it. I chew the bit of rind while I work lemon juice into the infection on my leg. The stinging in my fingertips and leg, electric, my nerves jumping and firing random muscles in response. The taste of bitter pith between my teeth nearly sweet and I swallow the ground up peel.

The water still has not come back on. I try to stand and find my leg in so much pain that I figure I better wait a little while longer. Just until I have some water. I sit staring at the branches moving and curse them. I curse them all, all the way from here in every direction to civilization. Where is everyone? I wonder aloud even though I know. This is an industrial farm run by robots and corporate executives. If there were any laborers out here harvesting on a typical day in this part of the season, they would have had their hours cut by the corporation to save on payroll. The fruit is not going to sell because the restaurants are all closed. The lemonade stands are all outlawed. The grocery stores are full of people obsessed about toilet paper.

I feel a rumble in my lower intestine. I drag myself over and away from the water hoses and pull my pants down. I try to squat on one foot but nearly pull a muscle and fall over. Quickly I aim my legs uphill, push my hands into the dirt to get as much lift as I can. What comes out of me might have been the entrails of a coyote having snaked their zombie way through my system, turning me rancid as they went. There are odd chunks of unidentifiable meat drained of color, but most of it is just watery filth. The backs of my hands are covered in this grime and the splash-back from aiming this jet of feces point blank at the ground covers my backside in a spray of indelicate matter.

Just as I begin to let loose with my diaphragm, the stream from the irrigation starts up again and I drag my shit covered ass back over to the dug up spot where the spring gushes forth. I lay on my side and dip my face into

Lemons: In an Orchard

the arc of laminar flow. I guzzle now and don't worry about puking. I am going to take whatever this little tear in the earth will give me. It feels like my last chance.

When it is over. I have a belly full of water and a body covered in a sheen thicker at parts and thinner at others, of my own decomposing innards. Once again, I hoist myself up and grab lemons off the tree. I take all my clothes off and mash them around inside the wet hole in the ground. I juice the lemons onto my flesh and clean the shit off. My sinuses are a sewer and an open grave.

With my wet and muddy clothes back on, and a lucky stick found beneath the tree, for a crutch, I hobble on. I am going to make it. It doesn't matter what happens getting there. I can suffer any amount of indignity. Any amount of torture, knowing that I will eventually be home safe in my own life once again. I will even manage to enjoy all the attention forced upon those in serious recovery from illness or injury. What do they call it? Convalescence. I will submit to convalescence. I'll allow myself to be doted upon. I wonder if Lisa even dotes?

I think I might lose this leg. I head toward a sunset I know is there somewhere behind a synthetic orange red sky. A cough from my lungs and a pain shoots up from my ankle and radiates into the shredded tips of my fingers. The coyotes worry me. I am not in the same shape I have been the last two nights. I am in decidedly worse condition. If they come for me again, when they come for me tonight, I'll have to pick a good tree.

Intestinal Discomfort

I look for any sign of difference between the trees and their branches which could translate into, better for fending off a coyote attack. The glow in the sky grows more luciferian red as I stare into a yellow orb hanging six feet away. It is as if the mountain forests caught the sky on fire. I find myself under a tree looking up. I'm not sure why, but, exhausted I begin to climb, dragging my leg up behind me. The pants have dried, the jacket is still a little wet. When I reach the top I pull it off and hang it to dry. The air feels cool on my skin. The temperature has been dropping at night. I might even die of mild exposure in my condition. Then the coyotes would have to eat me as scavengers. The vultures will come down eventually too. That was them up there circling, I'm almost sure. My stomach is sour and empty. The light is all gone. My bruised arms find their snug spots among the crooked stems. Skin feels the abrasive bark biting. I am getting used to discomfort, as for the third night in a row I have a branch between my legs.

6— ATAQUE DE EPILEPSIA

The coyotes did not come last night. Something else happened instead.

I waited for them. Exhausted, I started shivering and put the jacket back on, a little damp, but drier for the effort. I listened until I lost consciousness. My body propped in a convenient arrangement of notches. I slept and I dreamed about highways. I was in a car. I was in transit in this car. Driving on these roads that would jerk skyward into pointlessly high bridges over nothing, just a lot of grass below. The effect was like a roller coaster though. I was not enjoying it. Then the road came to another rise and it just kept increasing in angle until I felt as though I were going to slip out the back window or the entire vehicle would up and end over backwards falling some fathoms to a fiery fatoom. It stopped rolling forward. It began to roll back. Instead of going back the way I came, the vehicle sank backwards into an ocean. I swam to the surface and looked down through the clear blue salt water. There was my car, and my briefcase spilled open and all my papers on the ocean floor. Everything else was down there too. My bank account, my real estate portfolio, everything. I looked around and found myself standing in waist deep water. There were a lot of people playing on some kind of beach. There were strange water features everywhere and also, there were beings of a sort. They were waves, standing some three hundred feet tall. They didn't crash or move like waves at the beach. They were narrow, like columns of water with white caps at the top. I came near one of them and found myself pulled inside it. I rode up inside this wave on a shaft of light. The sun was out. It was a clear day.

When I wake up, the first thing I note is a scent on the air. It wakes me up actually. Like a room full of young women freshly showered and wearing clothes washed in lemon soap. I am groggy and wary of falling. My eyes are a bit unclear. Everything seems white. Like it has snowed. I blink and inhale again. It isn't snow. It's flowers. All the trees are in bloom. I look around and can find no more fruit, just flowers. My stomach feels like I

Lemons: In an Orchard

have swallowed a fish hook that has caught in my intestines and I am now being reeled in. My head swivels 180 degrees in either direction repeatedly until it makes me sick and I have to stop and breathe. At first, the syrupy thickness of the smell makes it difficult to find my breath. And I feel hungry again for the first time since vomiting up dog entrails the previous morning.

I climb down slowly from my perch. My leg is still a mess. My fingertips yet bloody and destroyed. I have not been miraculously healed. But, something has happened. Bees fly about everywhere. They are smacking into me and rolling around in the grass stunned and goofy, legs covered in so much pollen they look like little flying lemons themselves. I am so taken aback by the scene at first that I fail to notice the sky. A big yellow orb burns through its arc clean across the southern edge of a sapphire blue sky.

It is warmer this morning than it has been since I first found myself in this grove. I cannot explain what is happening to me here, other than perhaps I am delusional and lying in a ditch somewhere getting my guts eaten out by a cadre of monster dogs. I close my eyes and squeeze my face, trying to feel canines ripping my flesh somewhere in time, but, nothing. I open them and the sun is still shining and warm. The flowers are still white, like a blanket. The edge of the spectrum of all visible light, a vanguard against darkness, here I am. The smell is of the sweetness of fruit and fresh blossoming curiosity. It is an intoxicating thick atmosphere of nectar. There are trillions and trillions of these little white stars. There are so many of them the air resonates with them.

In my head a calliope sings a demented tune. On the ground, under the tree I find a watering can. It is heavy and made of sheet steel. Large, several gallons of water. The water in it tastes of a metallic urge to industry, but it is softened by the inescapable odor of the lemon flowers which becomes thick enough to taste in my mouth when I open up to drink from the can. Its edges are folded and softened. The metal is cool against my lips. The liquid feels silver in my throat. It tastes again of the can and the flowers, but also of something else which I don't feel qualified to describe.

I collapse into a lump under the tree. Cradling the water can I curl into a ball and cry. This can't be real, and even if it is real, what does this mean for my life? Yesterday, I was lost in an unknown location. Today, if all signs are to be believed, I am now lost in time-space, something so vast that all but the most esoteric scientists have avoided the idea of cataloging it. This is the type of vast dislocation in the hierarchy of being that prompted religion to develop. I lay on my side, clutching the can. The bees float around beneath the canopy like fairies tending gardens. The light breaks into shafts of gold among the fluttering leaves and the pixelation of the flowers. The steam organ in my mind drones on in an off-key high register and I remain floored by the impossibility of what has happened to me.

Lemons: In an Orchard

I believed it when I was abducted. It made sense to me that one day that might happen. and everything since then, up until this, has been a horror, but it's been a believable horror. A part of me knows I deserved it. I haven't been completely honest. You know I'm not a doctor. I told you I was an executive from a board of angel investors. That I bought and sold lives by the thousand. I didn't tell you everything, and I don't plan on it. What I will say is that waking up to a grim masque of death staring me in the face was something I had been used to for years. There wasn't much changed on that first day in the grove except circumstances. It was a different place, same old grim story.

People bother me. I don't like human beings. They are simple and dull and dishonest without creativity. They always expect to be taken care of, as if that's my responsibility and not theirs. Go out and work for it, I say. And if the company you are working for gets liquidated, roll up your sleeves and work harder. We can't all win. That's the capitalist way. That's the burden I bear. I'm the winner.

I get up from the grass where I have crumbled like a paper bag. I may not understand this yet, but I have to go on. Somehow this beauty is more horrible than the way things were yesterday. Like it's all a big tease. Any minute now the veil will be pulled back on the murderous glare of yellow eyes and teeth dripping with my already eviscerated guts. I'm dead and I don't know it.

That's all this is. It's so cruel. But I'm not one to hide from things. I harden up and pull myself up on my crutch.

The path between the trees is wide. The fruity ether glides down this channel. It is gentle and full of short grass. I take off my sneakers and let it touch my feet. Carefully stepping to feel out any obstacles at first. Finding none my pace becomes quicker, if not a little hobbled. The jacket begins to smell fecund in the hot sun. I look under the tree nearest me and see another watering can. Incredulous, I look around to see who is following me. There are bees. Some small songbirds. The rabbits as usual thought they were invisible until I looked at them square. Then they freeze as if accused. I lope under the tree and take my jacket off. Rinsing it as best I can, I wring it out and sling it over my shoulder. The water is cool and it pricks my hot red skin, running in tiny rivulets down my back.

There is something on the other side of this row. I can see a solid still form through the leaves. I poke my head out through the flowers and foliage. It is an empty work station. My stomach leaps. Hanging from a hook on a pole attached to a sawhorse are a pair of overalls and also a table and several implements.

I crawl entirely out of the thick and make my way cautiously over to the setup. The overalls are dusty and warm. There is another watering can on the bench. At this point, if anyone catches me bathing with their watering can and stealing their overalls, it will be a small thing in comparison. If they are even real. If any of this is real.

I can't help but dance as much as my injuries will allow, leaning into my crutch, awkwardly back and forth from my right to my left like an idiot. I strip. I wash delicately with the watering can. There is a rag on the bench and I use it to scrub my flesh. The stink of my open sewer cologne filters down off into the dirt and the perfume of the trees immediately clings on to me. My leg has not healed, but appears to be healing. The suppuration has dried up some. Golden crystals of calcified pus lined the scratches before I washed. The pink flesh cooled in the streams from the can and looked to be a shade lighter and cleaner.

When I'm finished, I sit with my dick out in the sun. The grass on my bare ass, I wait to dry. The sun continues to march across the blue dome above without hurrying. The scented breeze caresses my legs and I feel the hairs, escaping the grasp of moisture, aloft and swaying with the games of the wind. I put on the old overalls. They are soft and substantial. They feel as though they are a hundred years old. My jacket is dry and I place it over my shoulders to protect myself from the lancing rays of the fiery light above. I feel my face. The whiskers are coming in thickly. I know there is a good amount of gray in them.

I lift my palm and stroke my fingers through my hair, what remains of it. I had had the most luxurious blonde curls as a young boy. They had faded over the years to a light silvery brown. The follicles remained strong at the temples and the neck. They had weakened appreciably over the crown and my scalp is visible, though I have not gone completely bald. The overall profile of the coiffure remained somewhat intact as though my hair were a rug that had been lit on fire and quickly put out with a glass of wine. I am nearly an old man.

I feel like a scarecrow in my new stolen field hand outfit. The overalls are a little big, the jacket is still a little small. The denims are mismatched. The jacket wears tough through the abuse it has suffered still looks like it belongs at home in a shopping mall or at a discotheque on the back of a high seated lounge chair while its owner danced with the girls or got high in the bathroom. I look at the crutch I have been using. Something about it stands out to me as though in a new angle. There are the growth marks in a spiral around the body of the stick where a vine had wrapped itself, and later died and turned to dust and come off like some scab or crust. It left behind a symbolic shaft, which I had been propping myself up with for some hours now without noticing the pattern.

As I crutch forward the sun slips lower in the sky. It feels like a waste to let it go, and truly I worry to sleep here. I worry that anything I experience in this transformation will melt away in the dark and that I will awake back in that old world. That more real place where I was once a master of my life and of the lives of many others. That I will be transported once again to that realm

Lemons: In an Orchard

I know so well where I think I know how things work. I do not understand where I am, but find it preferable by miles to the world I have come from. Both lives seem like a dream and the likelihood that I will wake up in either of them and not in some locked ward in a hospital, suspect.

The light grows paler and somehow the scent of the flowers changes with the light. The trees recognize the shift and put on their night time cologne, even more seductive than the golden breath of the day time. This night cologne brings with it the whispers of nuance that can only be found in the dark where the feeling of touch and the odor of bodies and the sounds of sighs rule the senses. They know that as the bees become sleepy, the spaces within and among them will become a playground —or a carnal slaughterhouse.

I hear a drum. It is faint at first. It rises slowly over the darkening horizon and is joined by a troupe of others. They work at times in unison, at others they fill the empty spaces between each other or ramble all across each other. It is a primitive sound, but also the sound that evolution makes when it becomes aware of itself, begins to direct the flow of its own growth. I feel like I should be scared. How will these drummers take to a stranger? As hopeless as my life has become over the past four days, I have no choice but to investigate.

I follow the pounding with my feet, the clacking with my more sensitive eardrums. The sounds reverberate around the grove lost in the maze of reflective surfaces. Leaves twist upon being struck with the beat, as

though dancing. The sound glances off a leaf in motion
and twists in flight mimicking itself in two directions. I
have to feel out the lower waves coming through the
ground. My bare feet feel the tapping of thunder across
the earth and I follow my feet. The waves crawl up my
crutch and melt against my heart, which for the first time
in a while seems to be beating with some rhythm other
than the march of death.

I spill out across the grove in search of that
growing sound. Every hobbled step brings me closer to a
larger and larger sounding group. The timpani. The
bongos. The sticks flying in whiplash strokes. The
unmistakable sounds of voices calling out above this
riding and rolling sound, praying to gods I've never heard
of. Beseeching the future to come another day perhaps.
The sounds transport me a good quarter mile before I get
close enough to see what I have come so far only hearing.
I stop within a hundred feet of the sound and approach
with more caution, where my gut takes over and I feel
apprehension like a cold brick inside.

The rhythms pull me. I creep in under a lemon
tree to watch them closer. What I see is a village. There
are many small cottages made from wood, grass, and mud.
There are several larger buildings which appear to be
built out of a mixture of wood beams and adobe walls.
Lemon flowers are hanging in bunches everywhere.

The people are dressed in faded farm fashions
from the early twenty first century. There is plenty of
denim and innumerable patches sewn in place on knees

Lemons: In an Orchard

and across buttocks. Their bare arms ripple with every strike on the tightly pulled skins. Coyote furs cover their backs and chests. Some wear fur gauntlets. Well, that explains what happened to the coyotes.

Peering past the group which includes not just drummers, but dancers and revelers of all kinds, I can make out gardens in the purple dusk light. There are pens with animals. Chickens run loose among the stomping feet, heckled back and forth by the toes of the boisterous group. Pecking at them in return when a foot comes too close, squawking and flapping when kicked by accident. Torches burn yellow and orange around the center of the action.

I think my hiding spot is pretty good and that I will have some more time to watch. Perhaps I can discern a little more about the overall temperament of the group. A casual anthropology while laying on my belly under a bush. I don't want to find out through experience if they practice any form of ritual sacrifice. They killed the coyotes, that does not mean they are my allies.

I am thinking all this when I realize they have not killed all the coyotes and that my gaze as it passes over and through the crowd has become locked in the hypnotic glare of a dog crouching at the feet of a child. How long we have been gazing longingly into each other's eyes? I don't know. As soon as I clock it, the spell is broken and that dog comes charging after me. My stomach flips.

I am too weak yet to run. Quick as my arms can pull I go right up the tree over my head. This dog does not follow me into the branches but just stands below whining and making a sound that I suppose is meant to be a bark, though it comes off as more of a retching noise by my standards. It gathers the necessary attention from the group and several people come over to the tree. They are not shy about climbing it. I say, stay back. The dog growls up at me. I say, shut up dog! The dog gets quiet and there is a lone giggle from one of the children.

They murmur to each other while taking me in visually. It sounds a bit like Spanish. Eventually they all climb down the tree and go back to the village. A good sign. Then they set out a watering can and a bowl on a small wooden table. There is a large wooden handle sticking out of the bowl. My memory flashes back to the coyote fur between my teeth. I decide that I will come down, but that I will not eat anything until I have woken up here at least one more day.

I lead my own way down through the branches with my good foot. The dog, now silent, waits for me at the bottom. When I hit the ground he growls, but a child makes a noise at him and he stops. I can see markings of the coyote genome. It has large pointed ears, and penetrating eyes of amber full of trapped souls. I come out of the tree and approach the group. The dog follows me from a distance of about six feet. The villagers give me space too but are more open.

Lemons: In an Orchard

I sit down and lean against a stump. several of them come and sit down near me. They offer me the stew, but my stomach once again turns and my face gives away my condition. They pull back a little with the bowl. Look at each other and say, whisky.

Whisky? I say.

Whisky, they reply to me. A woman in overalls much like mine and a coyote fur choker turns in her seat to face behind her to a group nearest a large round building on stilts. Whisky! she shouts.

Within a couple minutes they present me with their version of whisky. It is unlike any whisky I've ever drank, but it is strong. I sip at it and their smiles are warm.

De donde vienes? asks the stocky girl in overalls.

I say, I don't know. I thought I came from Malibu, but I'm not sure exactly how far I've come. Seems so far that Malibu might be a stretch. It is a lot of words. They hear Malibu and their faces tell me what I have already surmised. There is no more Malibu.

Malibu? She says.

I nod and take a sip of the whisky, which is more like a pisco flavored with lemon blossoms.

She looks at me and her expression tells me she feels pity for me. I suppose because Malibu is a doomed word and I don't appear to know it. A few of the children have been playing with something like a frisbee. They stop and come and sit behind the adults. One of them says, you speak English?

I feel that kind of relief one feels unexpectedly over the buffet in a European hotel when amidst all the bon jour and crepes somebody vocalizes a perfunctory howdy. I turn and looked at the boy. He has blonde hair and dark eyes. I say, yes, I speak English.

My grandmother speaks English, he says.

How long have your people lived here? I ask.

Grandmother came here just before the lights went out. When did you get here?

This morning, I say.

From Malibu? he asks.

No, I was in the grove for a few days before, but... I don't know how to describe to an eight year old what happened.

He says, but you came from the other place. Not before. Sideways.

I don't know, I say.

You did, he says. I can tell.

The whisky is doing its thing. It has a pleasant taste. Not too sweet, a little smoky but also delicate. I finish my cup and they bring me another one. The circle is composed of women and men. No one bothers to recite the tribal history for me. A man looks at me and says, you ate the coyote?

My stomach turns again. I did, I say.

This is good. You are here for a reason, he says. His clothes are different from the others.

Another voice says, did you see the Eagle?

Lemons: In an Orchard

At that point, exhausted from exposure, infection, starvation, and alienation, I succumb to what is later described to me as ataque de epilepsia. My head tips backward, my tongue shoots out like a dying fish, and I thrash so hard against the ground that a man has to hold my head while a much bigger woman holds my body still. They bring out the medicine woman of the tribe and she spreads herbs around me where I lay. She lights beeswax candles with twine wicks and sets them around me in a seven pointed star. She walks between worlds and around me all night long in a circle of prayer. All this I am told when I awake.

7— ¿QUIERES TU RELOJ?

I **slept for several days. In my sleep they had managed to feed me with honey water.**

The whisky had probably pushed me over the edge. I was moved from my spot on the grass into a hut and given a soft bed of hay and chicken feathers. They covered me with a quilt made from plastic grocery bags stitched together in a thick mat. In my fever I tried to take stock of the room. There didn't appear to be any electricity as there were candles used for lighting and no electric appliances could be seen. The furniture was wooden and rudimentary but felt like it was influenced somewhat by modern designs that had been copied, but not quite worked out. It all felt makeshift. I guess two and a half generations is not a long time to develop a culture. Somebody stayed with me the whole time, though I couldn't see her face, there was something in the way she moved that felt comforting.

The comfort of my companion was interwoven with a dystopian nightmare. I was driving late at night on the PCH. The skies were nuclear pink crystals and the road was a flat ebony bone inlaid with crushed skulls of cattle. The signs were all in a language no one had ever seen. I felt an urge to find a bathroom so I took the next exit. There was only one light bulb at night in the entire town. It hung over the windowless door to a saloon with a parking lot full of black shiny cars like beetles in hibernation. I turned the key off and felt the engine stop. The silence and stillness was primordial. The air was arctic and I could see my breath forming my words in the air before me. They were all gibberish and I felt like an idiot.

I opened the door of the saloon. It was dimly lit and full of shadows. I went to the bar. The bartender would not turn to look at me, but took my order with his back facing me. My drink appeared on the bar before me without so much as a twitch from the man behind the counter. I took it and looked around the darkened edges of the room for the door to the bathroom. I found it outlined in silver as though lit from behind by a spotlight. The drink in my hand turned into a tarantula and I shook it off and shivered. There was a cloud of laughter in the bar as though someone had just made the biggest joke.

I put my hand on the handle of the bathroom door and felt a vibration from within. The door swung open, the room behind me filled with light and dissolved entirely, violently, as though turning to dust in an atomic blast.

Before me was a room lit from a high ceiling with thousands of long fluorescent tubes. A massive factory floor full of rows of stalls for what looked like miles. Each one tiled in a warm light beige four inch by two inch subway tile with dirty white grout. The pony walls between the stalls varied in height as if in a fun house. Some of them were only about two feet tall and the separation seemed comical. The place was as full as a train station on a weekend. Men in suits roamed between stalls, talking as though they were content to spend their entire lives in this public restroom between realities.

I had the urge to piss, but every stall I tried, someone would come up to the door and talk to me through the panel, or if it had short walls they'd come over and try and start a conversation over the wall. I couldn't find anywhere there wasn't one of these bastards ready to engage me on some subject. They all had this peculiar plastic grin and would stand well within my bubble of personal space.

* * *

Lemons: In an Orchard

When I awake my hosts tell me I have slept for a week. I am very hungry and now quite convinced that I will not be served any more raw coyote by hallucinatory mistake. They bring me a bowl of soup and instruct me to eat slowly, which is difficult because I am starving, but the pains in my stomach after just one bite of the tasty concoction convince me to put down the spoon for a moment and wait for the wave of anguish to pass. After that they bring me a shot of more whisky. I look into the eyes of the woman who brings me these things and tears begin to form in my eyes. I feel a blurriness come over me. I'm not big on emotions, so I don't know exactly what is happening. Some kind of relief at my temporary reprieve from death at the jaws of mother coyote I imagine. It makes me uncomfortable to know I am such a simple creature.

A few days later, the boy, accompanied by his trained dog, comes to see me. They are a quiet pair. The dog sniffs at my bed, my feet. Then it licks my toes, which makes me groan. The boy looks at me, then at the dog and he says, perro, no. No lo lamas. The dog cocks its head the way dogs always do, which has got to mean something. It does not lamas me again. Instead it sits on the floor at mild attention should I make any regrettable moves.

The boy is about ten. He reminds me of my own son at that age. Willful, smart, not yet entirely destroyed psychologically by the divorce that was surely about to erupt in his little world. I wondered who this kid's parents are. Surely I have seen them among the crowds, though he seems to be an emissary apart and on his own. A boy king surveying his domain. I say, what's your name?

He looks at me. Puedes llamarme Mani.

Okay Puedes, I say. What's your dog's name? Que perro?

He looks at me like I am an idiot and had just said the most perplexingly stupid thing ever. In fact, he shakes his head and doesn't answer me. Instead he says, Abuela says you are troubled, that you come here from another universe, and that in that universe your spirit died a long time ago. Now that you are here, your spirit in this universe will come to claim you.

I didn't know you spoke such good English, I say, as though everything he had just told me were an exercise in a book.

Ah! he says in frustration. It's like talking to a child. The dog makes a noise that starts with a long whine and ends in a growl and a gurgle and a yawn. The boy looks at it and nods. It stands up and they walk out.

If he wants to come into my recovery room and make up stories, as elaborate as they are, he really should expect to be treated like a little boy telling stories. I may not know where I am, but I know what I know. I can smell food cooking and rouse myself to go and search it out. Not having eaten for almost two weeks I am quickly regaining my stomach for it. I find that they have folded my stolen overalls and placed them on a stool made from lemon-wood branches tied together with vines. Hanging

Lemons: In an Orchard

on the back is the denim jacket, still two sizes too small. I get dressed. There is no mirror and I have yet to see my face at all since I've been abducted. I begin to wonder if I still have the same one. The air is warm, the sun is beginning another trip across a cerulean vault. It is big and yellow. Its rays comb the back of my eyes and make what's left of my hair straighten up.

The village is quiet, but not still. There is a large cauldron bubbling in the center of everything. A small group of children are tending it and the fire. Another group is setting dishes, an acrylic set of bowls that look like they came straight out of a lunchroom cafeteria. Green and brown in the shades of disinterest. They begin ladling big scoops of breakfast porridge into the bowls and handing them out to passersby. No one seems to be forming any kind of chow line, so I just walk within a few feet of the cauldron and get handed a bowl. It is steaming hot. The porridge is golden and smells of lemon blossoms. I blow on it. There are no spoons for breakfast. I see everyone using their fingers to clean out the smooth plastic bowls. So, I do the same. It is sweet and heavy. I still have to eat slowly and by the time I can finish the mix is cold and stiff, but still fragrant and delicious.

After finishing, my head feels woozy and I sit down on the ground for a minute and hold my face in between my hands, with my elbows propped on my knees. It is an undignified position, but I'm not in any position to demand much dignity from my life at this point. I look around. Men and women are going to work.

84

The division of labor is not clear. I don't think they decide based on gender. The women are strong. The men are wiry. The day has begun.

I gather my stomach and head back into the threadbare sack I've been carrying them around in. I get my feet under me and stand up. I go for a walk. I can see the edge of town, sloping down this gentle hill, some miles of orchard below me. It looks like every other tree has been excised, probably for lumber or firewood. And there are plots of farmland devoted to other crops as well, tobacco, beans, tomatoes, corn. This is a fully functional post-industrial permacultural community. But what is the rest of the planet doing? I stop a man, about five feet tall, with a bag of tools in his hand. Excuse me, I say, what happened to Malibu?

Esta in la mer Pacifico, he says.

Que? I ask.

Terremoto big, he says.

When?

Cuando todo comenzó.

That's not helpful, I say. He shrugs and moves on. The boy and dog find me staring after him.

Hombre, he says. Abuela quiere conocerte. Ahora, vamos.

I say, I'll follow you, Puedes.

He scowls at me and turns to lead the way to a smallish hut in the center of town. Though it isn't any bigger than any of the others, it is brightly decorated with gifts: idols, effigies, charms of good fortune. Casita

Lemons: In an Orchard

Abuela, he says. He bows before the door and says loudly, Abuela, estamos aqui!

Ven, says a woman's voice from the other side of the door. He pushes it open and leads me inside. I duck as I cross the threshold. The inside is full of smoke. There is a bowl of incense burning and Abuela is smoking a joint. To my surprise she hands it to the child. He takes a big puff and hands it to me. I say, oh, no thank you. He makes his eyes bigger and pushes it at me again. I take it from him and pretend to take a hit. When I go to hand it back, he looks at me and shakes his head. So I look for an ashtray.

Abuela says, please, you smoke it. Your spirit is trying to find you.

Oh, that's what Puedes here said earlier, but honestly I'd rather if whatever you think is looking for me might take a little longer to find me. I'm not sure I'm ready for all that yet.

Puedes? she asks. His name is Mani. You don't speak Spanish very well, I remember that about you. You are also not a good man. You are not a doctor either. I look at her face. Something is familiar. I have seen this woman only a little more than a week ago, but she has aged about fifty years.

You are the pregnant girl, I say.

Yes, she says.

You couldn't have been more than twenty last week.

I was a teenager in your world.

Um, come on. Abuela, please stop with that. I'm not a moron! I know that somewhere in this cottage there are cameras hidden, and whoever put me here is laughing their asses off right now about how stupid I look being given the mystical treatment and swallowing every bit of it. Well, I'm not. So you can take that back to your employers, whoever they are. Whoever I pissed off enough to do this, you can fuck off. I know you're listening.

You are a moron, she says. The kid laughs. The dog, startled, looks around at him at her at me. I lift my eyebrows at it and it snarls at me. What gives, dog? The boy puts his hand on its back and it quiets instantly. I hear a noise from another part of the cottage. I hadn't been aware of another room, but apparently there is because from inside that room comes a short and wizened old man. He is wearing a gold Movado watch. He comes into the room and sits down and says, donde esta Waldo? Estoy aqui.

Waldo, you prick! You left me to die back there. Do you know what happened to me?

He waves my complaints away, says, sabes lo que nos paso?

I don't sabes nada, I say. A spray of spittle flies from my s's. My hands are shaking. A cold wire wound around the base of my spine. The dog has his head lowered and his eyes raised in my direction. Abuela has closed her eyes and seems to be meditating or praying.

Waldo says, ¿quieres tu reloj?

Shit, I say, keep it.

Cuando nos despertamos no estabas ahí.

My Spanish is terrible. Teriblay, I say.

He says when we woke up you were gone, says the boy.

I don't believe you, I say. None of this is real.

Quieres creer que los árboles cambiaron de la noche a la mañana, says Abuela.

Él cree que somos actores, Waldo says.

Los árboles son actores también, she laughs.

The boy says, que es un actor?

I figure that I have to move the plot of this ridiculous charade along. I say, what do you want from me? What do I need to do?

Nothing, says Abuela. Just wait.

I cannot just wait, somewhere out there I have a family and a life to return to.

Just wait, says the boy. Abuela is very wise.

Waldo picks up the joint from the platter I had set it on and lights it, inhaling deeply. He hands it to me. Solo espera y mira, he says.

I take the joint from his fingers. They are smooth from years of labor. Everything smells intoxicating. I put the joint to my lips and inhale deeply. This is the game apparently.

The kid says, let's go. There is someone who wants to see you.

Again? I say, but he is already on his feet and the dog stands up and puts its nose in my leg, prodding me.

Pushy animal, I say. It growls low and the boy snaps his fingers.

Hasta noche, says Waldo.

Hasta, says Abuela.

See you later, I say. Thanks for all the food and restorative care.

You are welcome, says the boy.

He takes me through the small village to a hut on the outskirts. It looks nearly like the others but sadder somehow. The boy says, Oi!

A voice of an elderly man rises from the other side of the plank wall. He coughs and speaks. Yeah, ven. The boy swings the door open on its leather hinges. It makes a forlorn noise like a lost animal. Sitting on a cot is my son. He is older than I by twenty years. He says, sit down papa, and points to a lemon branch chair next to the bed. I dither. I consider running again. Fleeing into the lemon grove, such as it is, and taking my chances with the coyotes, with the world outside this village, whatever has become of the earth I can live with, but somehow facing this man feels impossible.

He says, dad, sit down please. I need to talk to you.

Each foot feels like it is pushing through concrete as I walk toward the chair by the mattress. I say, Chet? What have they done to you?

Heh, he says, saved me, raised me up from a state where I felt forever stuck in the shadow of a man I could never please and who never seemed to recognize me for myself. But that's all water under the bridge, dad.

I blink. This is not my son. That much is obvious. This is some look-a-like brought in from backstage. I bet they think I'm some kind of easily broken simpleton, softened up by years of effete living, giving orders and sitting back on my ass. Being obeyed has never softened me. Let's see your birthmark, I say. He smiles, which I don't like.

You'll have to help me. I can't stand on my own, he says.

So they're gonna make me molest a cripple. So be it. I have nothing to lose at this point except a pair of overalls and a bedazzled denim jacket. I lean over his prone form and draw back his blanket. The smell of old man is strong and mingles strangely with the flowers which work their way into every crevice of this village. He's wearing a paper thin pair of hospital pants underneath. I swear he had the same pair in his twenties, used to bring them on camping trips to lounge around campfire in the evening. I say, you know what I'm gonna do next?

You're gonna pull down my pants and pick up my pecker. Maybe while you're down there I can get you to pull on it a few times, no one else will.

You are one sick fuck, I say. I pull the blanket back over his groin and sit down in disgust. If you are my son, how the fuck did you get here? I ask.

Well, that's simple dad. Those people, whoever it was you fucked over in your bid to be emperor of fucking Malibu or the West coast or whatever, they picked me up the day before they got you.

Thoughts raced through my head. Lisa and the girls. What about Lisa and the girls? I asked.

That is just like you. You never gave a fuck about me. Did they torture you Chet? Did you get in any good kicks Chet? Nope. All you care about is the women, who you can't stand in person any more than anyone else, but they offer a convenient distraction when I'm around.

Boy, you are bitter. Come on, what about Lisa, and the girls?

You see those people out there?

Who?

The fucking villagers dad.

Yeah, of course.

We're all related kinda.

You don't mean...

I mean that most of them are your grandchildren in one way or another.. or both.

What do you mean, both?

I mean when things got real isolated around here we all got very familiar.

Fuck you. Where the fuck is Lisa?

Listen dad, I'm seventy-seven years old. How old would that make Lisa if she were still alive?

What about the girls?

Lemons: In an Orchard

Tammy died from coyote attack twenty years ago. She lived a happy life and had lots of babies by every man in this village who was of age at the time. Cherie lives in the village. Though she barely knew you when she was abducted. It's funny how these abductions were meant to destroy our family, but they only ended up preserving it when the rest of the global system fell apart.

Are you saying that there is nothing anywhere else? That we are the last family on earth?

I'm saying that we've seen others, but they weren't always coherent, and they weren't always human.

Not..human? I ask as though he has gone too far and must know it. Expect me to believe one unbelievable thing and then everything else though fantastic and unbelievable will be true by default.

You know what dad, I'd like you to fuck off for a while now.

You can't just drag me in here... I begin to protest but I'm cut off by the kid and the dog, who growls at me as if it knew English and were an avid conversant. I look at the dog and say, hey, cut it out, dog. To my surprise he snaps his jaws at me and lunges a bit before the kid smacks him on top of his head and he retreats, angry. I look at the boy. There is something inescapable about him. He is three and a half feet tall. He has furtive eyes like an animal, but they are also intelligent. I wonder, would he be my great grandson?

They escort me outside. I say, what now? I'm getting rather tired from all this meeting people.

He motions me to follow him. We stop outside another hut. He points to the door. Rest here, he says. With that, he walks away with the dog. The animal looks back over his shoulder at me as if to make sure I do what I am told. I give it the finger, half expecting it to run back over and bite me for my insolence. Fuck you dog. You should see what I do to dogs, dog. I'll eat your fucking intestines, dog.

I go inside. The hut smells strongly of the flowers, as though they had been used to cover the scent of a death. I mean, why else would there be a conveniently empty hut right here in the center of town if someone hadn't died. I wonder for a minute if it was Lisa.

8— DEMON RESPIRATION

find yet another watering can, full of this same pure water.

I drink a cupful. I haven't seen a river or even a stream, and I wonder where they were getting the stuff from. I am about to lay down to rest when I hear a knock on the door. That's weird, nobody seems to knock around here they just shout through the paper thin walls like some vaudeville act. I open the door and it's the guy from the drum circle. The guy who knew about the coyote buffet I'd had the morning before I woke up here. He says, you gotta talk to me.

I say, I'm a little fucking exhausted man.

Yeah, but, we gotta talk. We are from the same place, man.

Okay, well, damnit. Come in, I say and step back from the doorway. He does and I shut the door behind him. We sit at a table and chairs that look like they grew out of the ground, mostly I think because the table definitely did grow right out of the ground. It is a tree stump with about two hundred rings in it.

Out in the fading light of the doorway he looked about my son's age. A man, but still a boy by comparison. Chet would hate me for saying it that way. Inside, by the candlelight, his face looks hard, a youthful demagogue portrayed in effigy. The light from the candle tries to play with the shadows and the contours of his face. He looks evil.

He is dressed differently than the others, than me. He is wearing all black tactical gear. He smells like death. I cough a little at the eminence of his odor, even over the flowers. He sits like a mercenary, knees spread, arms gripping the chair as if ready to thrust himself out of it. Why do you think you're here? he asks. Watching my response with intense scrutiny.

I think someone is fucking with me, I say confidently.

Well, if they are fucking with you, they are fucking with me, and I'll tell you, that's simply not possible, he says.

I don't know, maybe you're an asshole too, I say.

Look man, he says. I kidnapped you.

I stiffen a little, remembering the press of this man and his group squeezing me into submission and unconsciousness. I feel like I should murder him, or at the very least kick him out of my new hut. What do you want then? I ask.

I'm not here to hurt you today. These coyote people. They aren't what they seem or what they say they are.

Okay, that much I knew. But, what are they?

I..don't know, he says, looking frustrated, turning his head to the right and looking at the wall.

Look at me, I say.

Man, I got nothing to hide. I picked you up and brought you out to this grove just like we were told. Something happened that was.. not to plan. You woke up before we'd marched you all the way to the spot. You bolted. I gave chase. I never saw my guys again after that. I didn't catch up with you either. I spent a night out there with the coyotes. I had my knives and I killed a few of them. They left me alone after that. I felt like a hunter, like a killer, man. So, I ate some of their meat, raw, you know. I thought I could own its soul. I don't think that's the type of soul I was meant to possess. The next day when the sun rose, I was in this place. They been treating me like a guest ever since man but things aren't right. Do you get the feeling like this is too perfect? Like where do they get all this water from? What happened to the rest of the world? Why is everyone still here after fucking fifty years? You'd think, well, like if the world ended, and you were in a lemon grove, would you just stay there? Would you build a village here? I mean wouldn't you move around a little bit first?

I don't know. I have felt like they were a part of some ruse by my kidnappers to torture me. I honestly don't believe any of this is real.

Shit, man. I'm one of your kidnappers, and I'm not no grunt either. I wrote the plan. But, this is not in the plan I wrote. Lemme ask you something.

Shoot, I say, before realizing he probably has a gun.

You are a pretty bad dude. We didn't pick you out of a hat, here's your lucky bad day in hell stranger. You're an evil man.

That's not really a question.

No, it's not. Me, I'm a bad man's nightmare, someone who loves making em' squirm. You love money and power, yeah?

That's right.

I love murder, chaos, and the smell of the fear of my enemies.

Charming, I say.

You aren't supposed to like me. But I think you and I need each other right now. I don't want to be stuck in paradise unless I'm in charge. I don't know what these guys have for warriors, but I'm surprised nobody has come in here already and murdered the lot of them. What do you say we make a pact. Let's have a coup on that old Abuela and her cuck Waldo. I don't know how they been in power so long, but I got a feeling it's based on a lack of challengers.

I suppose you aren't gonna let me think it over.

No, you know that much, he says, head leaning forward, eyebrows lifting, staring me dead in the eyes. No, he can't let me live if I'm not on his side. Can't risk me letting them know his plan.

What if I do help you? What is my position in the new hierarchy?

You'd be second in command after me. I know these are supposedly all your grandchildren, but if you don't believe that anyway, guess it can't hurt for you to enrich the breeding stock a little. He says this, then he smiles like a true psychopath.

Okay, what's our plan then?

It's the dog, he says.

What? That fucking spastic angry coyote with the kid?

That one.

And?

That dog is the center of it all.

So, we kill it?

Yeah, we do. And the kid too. They're one and the same creature.

I don't understand.

I been watching people around here. They ain't all people. That kid, that dog, ain't a human being.

Now you are starting to sound as crazy as the rest of them.

That's fine, he says. Just keep an open mind and do what I say.

Okay, I say, and I stand up and put out my hand.

He grabs my outstretched palm with a steel grip to seal the deal. I'm old. I'm also a little torn up by spending five days living off of water from an irrigation system and eating coyote intestines, translate:dog shit. I'm also a rank-less member of a specific nameless art. I practice arts known to only a few men, and this guy, tough as he is, isn't one of them. He doesn't even come close. I do something with my hips, push and pull him a touch to feel his equilibrium. It's just as I thought, he's locked his sacral vertebrae in some kind of macho wingding spread em' posture. I pull him right over the table, which is very sturdy, as it is made of solid tree trunk rooted into the soil floor. Thunk! I nail him in the face with the half-full watering can. He is trained well, doesn't make a noise as I compress his ribs against the edge of the table while disarming him of his weapons, which I find all over him. He continues to struggle of course, but once I have one of his knives, it comes to a swift and bloody end.

I manage not to ruin his tactical gear. It gets a little bloody, but at this point, human blood has become innocuous in comparison to the things I've been wearing. He's about my size, a little thicker the way younger men are when they are lifting regularly, which also happens to make them stiff and easy to throw around a room.

After stripping the body and wrapping it up in the hand woven fiber rug from the floor of the hut, I lay back on the cot and rest. My eyes flutter and close. I have never been at peace and have always managed to find some kind of sleep very easily, and other kinds not at all.

✳ ✳ ✳

In my dreams, Abuela comes to me. She tells me that the reason I am displaced is that my spirit is fractured. I walk on through the hellish dream-scape, patio furniture clinging to my legs, overhead shadows blot out the nether sun. Bricks form walls and tunnels that look like buildings and streets at a glance, but further inspection reveals them to be simply puzzles and doors to more twisted realms. I come upon a demon seated with its back to me. In one hand it grasps the skull of a young child. It has the child's face buried entirely within its dark demon lips. The boy's body inflates and deflates with the demon respiration like a paper bag over the mouth of a hysteric. I walk past and see high distorted cheek bones, a forehead like a white anvil. I feel the sucking out of eyes and breath. Watch the rising and falling of the shapes, one into another. Some kind of dark spirit parasite drinking the life breath of the child. They may even be symbiotic at this point. I can't tell, and I'm not going to pull them apart.

I walk on past the powdery pale neck and arching spine in black burlap suit heaving and sucking on that little body. Next I come upon another pair. This time the boy is in adolescence. He is screaming a choking lament as the arm of a torturer presses down into his body through the throat. It's trying to jam something inside him, or pull something out. The boy is damaged and twisted. His lips are torn open at the corners from being stretched by the nearly sexual onslaught of the demon. I see it pull now, and out comes some human remains, a fistful of jawbones and teeth, glistening with ectoplasm and blood. Sharp like a grip of macabre knives. The boy sits and vomits into his hands. He looks at me but doesn't ask for help. The demon focuses solely on him.

I walk back into the room with Abuela. She says, you are forgiven. I can't help but see you in all my children and grand-children.

✻ ✻ ✻

I wake up shivering. It's not cold, but there's some adrenaline from the fight being burned off. I dress in the other guy's gear. Now, I'm armed. I am not helpless anymore. I walk outside and the sun is setting. The sky is lavender above a fog of white flowers. Bees are rushing home. An eagle flies across the sky from left to right. I go looking for Abuela.

I find her and Waldo at the center of town. They are blessing the evening meal. They tell me to sit down and eat, which I do. The stew is the same stew we've been eating since I got here. How long has it been now, a week? They don't ask me about my clothes, which is telling. This is a small community, surely they all noticed the change and the absence of the other stranger. Only the kid, who swaggers up to me with his dog, says, nice clothes.

Thanks Puedes, I say, reminding him he's still a little shit.

I sit next to Abuela and get right down to it. Look, I say, if you don't tell me what is actually going on here, who hired you? Where am I? and How do I get out of here? Bad things are gonna start to happen around here, and I don't think you people are ready to handle it.

Hmm, she says, as though disappointed. Didn't you get my message? From the dream?

I say, look, I don't know what kind of advanced psy-ops you are running here, but I got a feeling that if I start sinking knives into people you'll be dropping the act pretty quickly. I would rather not do that.

At least you are consistent, she says. One of the answers you seek, you will find at the river.

What river?

Mani will take you.

Fine, but tell him to leave the dog behind.

He cannot. They are inseparable.

If I kill the dog?

That will not go well for you. Mani likes you, despite yourself. He will not allow the dog to hurt you.

That's reassuring, I say with my best and most serious sarcasm.

Finish your meal, it won't do you any good to go hungry, she says. And I do.

9— START LOOKING INSIDE

After dinner Mani finds me again. The dog has a strange look on its face which I don't **like.**

First of all I don't like that a dog can have a strange look on its face, second, the look seems to be like that of someone who knows a secret, who knows that you don't know, and who knows that you know that he knows and that you do not. She looks smug for a dog. Her yellow eyes are anticipating my chagrin at something. I say, taking me to the river at night, Puedes? He shakes his head as it's a waste of time to answer me.

You see. This river is special, he says.

It better be, I say.

Or what? he asks. I am surprised to be confronted by someone so small, but then remember he speaks for the dog as well.

I say, you'll see. I don't feel particularly threatening though, and he doesn't look particularly concerned. The dog still smiles queerly.

Follow me, he says.

I figured as much, I say. I follow him and the dog out the door. We walk back the way I had come from when I first entered the village. I say, how far is it? I already came from this direction and didn't see a river.

He shushes me. Now I can say I've been shushed by an eight year old and his murder dog. I shush, but mostly because as a conversation partner, these two are not very engaging. We walk for about a mile or so. The terrain is easy and my leg has healed quite well. I still carry my crutch, but it has become more of a cane or staff. A primary means of defense against whatever is out here in the dark, though it appears to just be me, the boy and psycho-mutt.

He stops at the end of a row of trees. I hadn't seen the end of a row before, and it is notable for one to suddenly appear. With his back towards me he says, Abuela says you're sick. She says you are possessed by an evil spirit, and that we shouldn't trust you.

What do you think? I ask.

I think you're a retard, retard, he says.

Excuse me?

That seems to be the most appropriate term I have found in your vocabulary. You think you have been ahead this whole time, but actually, you've been very far behind.

I feel like he's toying with me now, and I start looking around for the hidden hand, coming to humiliate me with a strike from behind or above. But I also stop walking, and I listen. The sound is like a chorus of paper shredders waltzing uphill. It's a river and it's not small either. Apparently I missed it somehow in my fugue state upon first arriving.

He's standing on the bank above a rushing black line. The moonlight fractures into quanta and is delivered as if on conveyor, downstream. This moment is being washed and washed away in time. His back to me, smug and proud. Reading my mind, hmm? I doubt it.

I walk silently up next to him and push him in. The dog leaps at me. I spin and uppercut it in the tits while simultaneously tossing it overhand into the current. They both disappear silently beneath the ink black depths and surly white cap turbulence. I stand with my back to the grove and contemplate the motion below me. The river makes a peculiar type of silence by drowning out everything around it in white noise. I feel peace, like I've finally found some place safe. I hear Mani and the dog walk up behind me. That was quick, I say.

Yeah, we didn't really go anywhere, you know.

I turn around and look. They are not even wet. Is that really water?

Is anything really anything?

I suppose you've got a point, I said. What happens if I go in it?

That's what you're here to find out, he says, and runs at me with his palms out.

I find that I don't want to get out of his way. It is clear to me now, this whole thing is beyond my control. The dog howls in tune with the white noise of the river, somehow making the rushing sound of the water grow as Mani closes the gap between us like a bolt of light. I do the only thing I can. I drop to my knees and spread my arms wide.

Our chests thump together and I realize that he had dropped his hands and encircled my rib cage. I wrap my arms around him and stand up. The damned dog is at my side. It licks my pant-leg. I lean back carried by the impact of his tiny body into an arc, falling end over end, down into the darkness and the cool loneliness of that river. I wonder where I will wake up, and when.

We disintegrate in that flow. I become time itself and look upon twelve generations of my grandchildren. How they veer and vault along their lifelines, each one moving closer to or further from my path. Some are criminals, street drunks, others teach kindergarten, make sandwiches for the homeless, travel the earth far and deep. There is a psychologist to whom I appear as a spirit.

Lemons: In an Orchard

There is a woman whose life consists of cutting flowers and masturbating in the tub while listening to jazz. She has a greater connection with the silence and solitude than anybody I have ever encountered. I see a little girl, age ten, wearing a pageant outfit covered from head to toe in vomit. Her mother stands by, looking like she could burst into tears or laughter. The girl also on that ambiguous perch.

That moment of recognition of the bodily nervousness of being, combined with the divine comedy of life, supported and nurtured by a warm and loving family, branching out, her life takes a turn away from seeking validation from external approval. She becomes a much more inwardly driven being, an artist. She will never be satisfied by earning credits, whether they are dollar signs or the lustful stares of men. Those things will just be color in her world. What moves her from then on is explosive emittance, spontaneous dance, paints on a canvas, music in her ear, the magic of edible spell-crafting, and the warmth of true friendship through adult to adult conversation and energy transfer.

There is another little girl whose mother, barely a child herself, would drag her around town like a sidekick, into all the bars and the backyard parties. The girl feels like an adult. Watching her mother charm herself and the men around her. Even standing guard outside the door when mom wants to get with one of her boyfriends. At twelve, she learns that adults do whatever they are compelled to do to feel okay, even though it means that her father, working eighty hours a week, comes home to an empty house, makes himself a TV dinner. Watches TV alone. Tries not to think about where his wife and daughter are. Jerks off silently to barely legal web-porn. And then stays awake until early hours waiting for them to come home, for his wife to get in bed with him, her comfortable mountain shape smelling of parties and sex, when he will finally hold her and be able to sleep, requiring little of her, but her presence for a few scant hours of rest before they all get up and do it again. That girl's sisters all have different looks to them. Her father's genes are strong, but not always present.

A boy, whose father left his life at one year, now three, talks to himself in the dirt driveway of his home. He swishes a crow bar back and forth in the dirt. Bare feet sensing the magnet beneath him, the tickling of life between his toes. He's making up stories about someone he can't consciously remember. They are stories he doesn't really understand, but they drive him to rage. His forearms at three are like the arms of his father, supple, but hard as tree trunks. The crow bar rises and falls in great arcs, over and again, in a murder of a pristine lawnmower borrowed by the mother from the boy's adult sister from another mother. Nobody for miles is present to hear his pain. The mother is passed out on the couch. The neighbor is a deaf couple. The trees surrounding the home are indifferent to such momentary bursts of animal emotion. They have, after all, bears using them for scratching posts.

Lemons: In an Orchard

Another man, secretly gay, goes into a tobacco store. He's got a boyfriend at home, though he has another secret, a crush on the young man who works at the store. He brings in a book to give to him. It's about the blues, as a musical genre, as a psychological phenomenon, as a depth to which some aspire, and a hole from which others cannot escape. He looks the younger man in the eyes, he doesn't stray, down his long arms, to his washboard stomach exposed by a ripped half shirt, to his butt in those torn punk rock jeans that haven't been washed or changed in six months. He just keeps eye contact, quietly smelling the man's body odor, which to so many people is offensive and brutish, but is nothing short of aphrodisiac to the keeper of secrets. He gives the younger man some authentic engaged conversation about music, about life, then he goes home and shoots himself in the head, quite efficiently. When the boyfriend calls, estranged after several weeks of non-stop arguing, the phone just rings and rings.

I see a man in a studio space filled with paintings. He is obsessed with pulleys and rigging and has set everything up in the place to ride on track and be pulled aside, along, or aloft effortlessly with a carefully balanced set of counterweights, wheels, bearings, and strings or cables. It is a bit like a mechanical spiderweb, but instead of everything sticking to it, everything just slides around on it. When he gets going, running around the space like the spider, he can flip with the tip of his index finger large sheets of plywood that come up and cover the windows for a projected transformation of the space, overlaying the darkness with a two dimensional picture that cuts across the aerial network of tram cables to splash upon a white screen, two dimensions becoming three, and three, two. He continues on his marathon around the space turning cabinets upside down with a glance to reveal hidden stashes of archived artwork, a pot of beans that appears through a hole in the wall. A magic floor that opens up revealing a clockwork center.

There is a man so alone and broken that his weight is like an unbreakable stone. He carries it around and uses it to justify his wickedness. It is so small that he can hide it inside his heart and it will never show outside, never come up in a cardiogram. He's perfectly healthy, they always say. At first, as a boy, he thinks other people might care. He brings it to his father and mother. They say, don't worry son, you just get used to it. In time you won't even notice. And at first he doesn't. Then he has a son who only ever wants his approval and can't get out from under the weight of his father's stone.

I recognize myself, though not at first. At first I just feel sad for the man. When I recognize my own face, it is in this mirror that I see myself for the first time, my complete lack of awareness of my connections to the world around me, spreading out and backwards and forwards in time. I see the actions of a helpless automaton, but I see something else too. There is self awareness, there is a spark, it is small and dim and neglected. But it is there, and that means that I had always had a choice. And that I let fear choose.

If I had had a body at that point I would have felt anguish. I would have clenched my fists and held them to the sky while crumbling at the knees. But it was just another moment in the universe. I was awash in the cosmic rays of the twelve dimensional lattice of hyper-time-space. I stayed there for an eternity.

* * *

When the river spits me out, I am once again sitting with Abuela. This time she is young again. We are under the tree where we had met. We are alone, the stars are out. She takes my hand. I look down and see that my hand is smooth and light brown. I lean into her ear. I kiss her just below it on her neck and she giggles but doesn't pull away. She places my hand on her breast and I feel the excited points beneath her shirt. Just cotton fabric between my hand and the ecstasy of her vibrant body. I become more aggressive and she lets me.

Her name is Katrina. Her hands are curious extensions of her mind. They pull at my clothes. They push at my body. My body is hard and twenty. I am not an expert, I just have guts. She pulls my shirt off and her hand traces sigils on my bare hairless chest. I wonder if it's something she sees, or something she's drawing out of me. I taste her neck with my teeth and she folds in my arms and moans. Heat shoots out of her body. I gently pull her shirt over her head, exposing twin beauties the size of lemons, with nipples the same shape and size as the tip of the fruit. They are olive white, the lines of her tan ending with the rippling foothills of her rib cage, the horizon of her collarbones. She pushes me hard onto my back and sits on top of me. I place my hands on her small hips. My hands seem large and hard, she is small, soft and delicate. Her spell casting returns to the subconscious drawing of charts and symbols on my chest. With every feathered stroke I become harder beneath her until I am sure I can't be held back. She draws a line finally down down down to my belt. Her hand undoes the buckle with considerable effort. I try to help but she shushes me and puts my hands back upon her bare sides.

My pants are off and she's on me. She is preparing me with her tongue. Her mouth is hot, insistent. She has one hand around the base of my cock.

I reach down to find her hand that holds her up. I touch her fingers. My fingers coax her attention to bring her lips to mine and she does. With her laying atop me like a mountain silhouette, I slip her pants and panties off. The musk of new dew fills my head and there is no way I could possibly be harder, but I am. I am frenzied for her magic.

She spreads her legs over me and leans in hard with her pelvis, pressing down on my cock with her swollen vulva. She takes me. I stroke her body atop mine until she finds her chi. In that moment she thrusts down upon me with vigor that rises up like the kundalini snake. Her moans and whimpers are calls to the unseen. I feel her body inside changing around me. She's coaxing me now. Her moment's come and she's looking for the finale.

I sit up, still inside her. She moans as I pull her, slide her up and down. We roll together. I'm on top of her now. She's bleeding a little bit. Her fingers use the fresh blood to paint my face and hers. I become animal. Biting and licking and groaning, growling. I fuck right through her and into the center of the earth. I feel my belly heating up and becoming soft with a charge building to blow. Her moans and shrieks coordinate in my mind's eye with the visualization I have of myself as being summoned, a long slumbering monolithic totem. I will cleanse the earth with my ejaculate.

When I come, I come so hard that I plow my forehead into the dirt repeatedly next to her face. I split my eyebrow on a rock. more blood gushes warm down my face. She licks it off my lips and bites them. There is a reddish black spot in the dirt from my bleeding skull. Her eyes are liquid, shining in the silver light from the moon and the cool breath of the stars. Her smile tells me that the spell was cast properly.

I look again at my hands on her body and we are old again. I am white and pale and my flesh smells like I've evolved to sweat old spice. She is perhaps the oldest woman I've ever seen naked. Her olive skin, smooth in spots, shivers into wrinkles at the extremities. I think, it's true, women only age from the neck up, the wrists and ankles down. She gets into child's pose and starts humming to herself. Her shape is that of a sketch made with a paintbrush. The round strokes of her ass, painted in umber, her shoulders with the knots of decades of casting and weaving, cleaning and nurturing, look like the shoulders of a DaVinci sketch, all cords and machinery buried deep under a sweet smelling cloth, soft to the touch above, impenetrable complexity below, an example of how everything connects and each tiny movement can be felt across the whole as a tremor, or a passing shadow.

I find myself reaching for her naked back. I lightly touch her with my fingertips, then press my palm more firmly onto her. She turns her face to me and I see it is filled with stars. Her mouth is a parenthetical smile, with her ear pressed to the ground. Her nostrils continue to constrict and dilate in a pattern of processing the steam coming off of her shoulders. Her eyes meet mine, the corners of them play little games with my attention. She is thoroughly entrancing. My hand moves across her soft shoulders and down the back of her rib-cage, over her sacral spine, and back again, as I begin to explore, just the terrain that she presents in that position, ass up tits down. I press my fingertips and knuckles into the various places I feel calling for attention. Hear her moans and sighs in response as she melts more under my touch.

She turns her forehead to the ground and takes a large in-breath. I watch her stomach inflate. Her wrinkles smooth as the flesh beneath them grows more hydrated and supple, expanding while the skin shrinks off it's age. Her belly grows into a roundness as she sits up. Her breasts, which were deflated and hanging without much sense, begin to swell and perk with the weight of milk. She stretches up with a tall spine onto her knees and heels. Her buttocks looking firm and fresh, her swollen stomach continuing to grow to term, belly button poking out like the nipple of a lemon.

I pick one from above our heads and show it to her. She laughs. She takes it and bites into it. I see her body shiver from the taste. I lean in to kiss her and she spits it playfully into my mouth. My body shakes from the act, both intimate and transgressive. I put my hand on her stomach. She laughs again, this time at my doctor joke. I feel a series of swift kicks coming from within. This baby must have six feet or the reflexes of a mantis shrimp; you know, those shrimp that can punch things to death.

I look again down at my own body. I have not gotten younger, or older. I'm just me, what I expect to be these days when I get up and look in the mirror every morning, checking the reflection for signs of death. Liver spots, crepe papering, bed sores, ulcers, streaks of poo from nocturnal incontinence. But I'm clean, if not restored to glory. My dick is swinging, deflated and a little tender still from Katrina using it as a magic wand. Why is everything so symbolic, so easy to ignore until it isn't? I sit close to her, my ass in the grass, blades mingling with hairs and tickling my nethers, wrap my arms and legs around her and hold her. She vibrates with affection and pours herself into me, leaning with a smooth face into my burnished chest. I feel something in my heart.

It's a defect. It's a weakness. It shoots right up into my eyes and they begin to water. My face makes a grimace like a wounded clown. I bare my teeth silently to the sky while she nuzzles further into my core. I make no sound as I feel this weight placed outside me by invisible hands, and I watch it blown away by the slightest breeze. How long has that been there? It felt so substantial, but really it was nothing.

The petals begin to fall like snow. Fruit forms, grows swollen and drops as well. by the time it hits the ground it has become dirt again, and is quickly swallowed up by the claymation grasses that swirl and sway but never outgrow their place. I feel them brushing our thighs like the lapping of waves in wading depth.

* * *

I remember a day at the beach. I was forty. We were building sandcastles. I had cool sunglasses, they were gargoyles, you know, cop glasses, tactical stuff that was big in the nineties. Darby was sunning herself. She liked to do that, just put on some oil and lay back in a lounge chair. She looked good back then, twenty seven years old. Two pregnancies behind her and fit as a model, not skinny like that, strong, and beautiful. I wanted to hold her forever. By that point things were already rough though, and the signs were there.

I helped Chet build sand castles, showed him how to plan for the incoming tide, build a moat, a flood wall. We used buckets and cups to form parapet walls, central towers zooming three feet into the air on a base of hard packed sand. We dug out tunnel entrances, courtyards, window openings. I found some scraps lying around on the beach and we made a drawbridge, and some peasant market looking area. On the top of the highest tower we put some effigies to our patriarchal line. There was me and him.

I felt like I was lying to him, or leaving something out, but I didn't know what, and he didn't seem to care at the time. He just kept talking out this fantasy world that he'd built up instantly in his head about this sand castle we were building. It seemed like he thought it would last forever.

Darby lay silent as the crypt, her skin glistening as it darkened in the afternoon sun. The beach bag by her chair filled with paperback novels, sun lotion, a sleeve of crackers, baby wipes, and a little weed dugout. I looked at her through my sunglasses. She was wearing her blackout Liz shades and I could not see if her eyes were open or not. I ran my eyes up and down her body, hoping for some sign in her face, some little smirk or smile that would show she noticed my interest. I didn't know what to say, so I just looked silently until I heard Chet saying, dad, dad, dad. She moved then. Lifted her glasses and looked at me. She didn't smile. She scoffed a little. Her eyes seemed to say, go on dad.

The tide was coming in. She sat up and said, what do you think guys? Time to go.

I said, yeah, I guess so.

Chet said, no, please mom, just ten more minutes.

That's an impressive bit of work there honey. The tides gonna come and wash that sandcastle away though, you don't wanna be here to see that do you?

No mom, we built it so it wouldn't. The waves can't touch it, he said.

I felt like I had somehow misled him into thinking that anything would last.

She said, alright babycakes, ten minutes more.

Mom, he said, I'm not a baby.

The first wave that got close ran away with the beach bag, which I chased down into the surf.

My bare feet in the cold water felt silent, enshrouded. The sand beneath my barely calloused soles was a cat's tongue. Small shells and rocks prickling and poking at my toes. I caught the bag. One of the paperbacks was wet, but that's pretty much why people bring them to the beach. They are hard to destroy, not very intricate text. You can pretty much lose a hundred pages and the thing is still just as readable. And if the ending is lost it was usually so predictable anyway that the average reader knows from the jacket what the outcome will be.

Lemons: In an Orchard

When I came back with the bag, dripping saline solution like an IV punctured in multiple spots, Darby was standing. She had dragged her chair up the beach and was watching me and Chet. He was standing inside the flood-wall, knee deep in water, face red and tears streaming down his hot little cheeks. Dad, he screamed, I thought we built it good enough!

* * *

When I look at Katrina, she is crying. She has poured out a hot wet ocean onto the silvery hairs of my chest. I look into her bright eyes and I laugh. She breaks into laughter as well. I kiss her forehead and she begins to age again. I look around for the child she must have birthed, I see a coyote pup, wet with afterbirth, standing with shaking legs trembling, with the fear and astonishment of everything that enters this world. Her small golden eyes searching for the warmth she'd just left behind.

As the wrinkles return to Abuela's forehead I watch her fade. The dog grows fast. She is strong and we play tousling games in the grass beneath the tree. I stay by Katrina's bedside until she passes. Her body glows and then turns dark. Leaves creeping up through her navel, between her arm and through her armpits. Eventually a tree grows out of her mouth where the sunlight creeps between the barely parted teeth of her savasana. It grows and replaces the tree we have spent our lives under. And it flowers in the spring, bunches of sweet white flowers that smell so intoxicating I know I would never leave. I cry at the base of her tree for a lifetime, while the dog runs around it in circles and howls on moonlit nights, calling mother, come back.

I look at my own mother, back in her faded photo sundress, standing in front of the house with that smile on. The one she always put on for the camera, which wasn't really much of a memory of her at all, which is really how it was. If I try to think about who she was, I can remember a woman who told me what the rules were, who corrected my behavior, fed me meals and answered my questions with an encyclopedic level of precision. She never showed the slightest bit of emotion. Not even when dad died. She just kinda kept on with lunch and tea and bowling on TV the way she had for the twenty years prior. Grandchildren were nice to look at. They were okay when they were running over your lap, but they didn't really do much for her. Katrina's tree weeps big transparent drops of nectar down from the flowers, covering me in a sugary dew.

My own hands grow roots as I sit back in the grass one day. The dog climbs up into my lap and licks the sap off my face. She looks into my eyes very close. Hers are yellow, mine are brown, still full of shit. We laugh. A yote boar comes around and they make puppies right there in my lap. The pups are all born blind and squirming little helpless crying dreamers. The parents stand guard over the fumbling movement. The yote goes out and hunts rabbits to feed the pups. He comes back with seven in one trip, collated on one giant canine. The parents grind them up and swallow the rabbits, then lean over the nest, which is beneath my branches and regurgitate rabbit stew into the tender mouths of the infants.

✻ ✻ ✻

I am laying in some dirt, under a lemon tree, looking up through the branches at the smoke filled forest fire sky of southern California. I have just about every external reason to live, to thrive. Why am I out here punishing myself and hoping to die? I guess I know. I know why I have done this to myself. I just don't want to admit it. It's all so obvious now. There is too much junk. I have to clean it out. I have to make myself into a functioning paper mill. I don't know any other way. I think if I just arrange things on the outside that they will all come together on the inside.

I think that about Darby, about Chet. I think that about Lisa and the girls, but really why does my relationship with them work if not because they stay out of my way? If I can just arrange the space, put things where they belong, I will be able to think clearly.

I walked out here from the highway. I left my car, my phone, my jacket, everything but my watch. I was looking for some peace. Some order. Some bitter reflection. I got lost. I've never been lost before. I've always known exactly where I was. Maybe there's something wrong. Maybe it's dementia, but I'm only sixty. Said every early onset Alzheimer's patient ever.

I was drawn by the spell of a young witch, but I wasn't even me. I was Waldo. I'm not even sure that I am me. The branches are laden with ripe lemons. No one is buying anything but toilet paper and art. It's not a good sign. The restaurants are filled with caution tape.

Booze and tobacco are up. Underground unsanctioned gathering spaces are at a premium. But, I hate gatherings anyway. I should be in heaven with this social distancing. I should be writing a new business plan, or learning Chinese again, or working out twenty four hours a day. I just can't sit and watch TV. And there is only so much space to organize. There is only so much stuff to throw out, externally. And then I have to start looking inside.

10— COVERED IN VISCOUS LIGHT

The branches of the tree are still. The lemon's ripe sour weight drags on down, but she can take it.

I remember how strong these branches are. The sun is coming up somewhere on the other side of a smokescreen. The world is lit fairly well now. A pink wan detached from any sense of softness. The rabbits will be running soon, having survived the fierce night buried deep in their warrens, snug together. A gopher pops up, his hands and head supporting a wedge of earth, like some sort of abstract backwoods Carmen Miranda. His hidden hips swaying back and forth in mesmeric rhythm inside his tunnel, his blind eyes searching the terrifying geometry of the horizon where smells travel like race horses across an open plain. Birds have been singing since before light. Determined to establish authority over the day by waking the others up, come on, you're missing it, you're missing it, they say.

My spine is propped against this old tree. A composition of numbness and itchiness, until I move. Until the blood regains its velocity and the nerves wake up, I'm basically a human pin cushion. The kids used to tickle me when I wasn't looking to see if I could feel. Looking down, my sneakers are like year old dish sponges. They still work, but at what cost to the system as a whole? They were white just last week, or whenever that was. Now they are washed in dried and hardened biological strata. I can see patterns in the stains that probably aren't really there. A dog, a river, an old woman, a knife. The torn open leg of my jogging pants where the dust and diffused sunlight have been accumulating on my thigh. Hand-prints as if marked in ceremony, like leopard spots or turkey drawings by grade school children, where I've smeared myself clean. An ankle, blistered and fever red, but not septic.

I haul my corpse to stand, or lean rather. The walking stick is nearby and I prop it again, under my shoulder, the goose neck top fitting snugly into my armpit. Funny, it just grew that way, then snapped off at exactly the right length and lay waiting on the ground for me to be happening by with a serious injury and need its assistance.

Outside the tree, I can see more trees. They are tightly packed together, lemons pressing upon lemons in a mono-crop cornucopia of what would amount to a whole lot of cleaning product now that the market shifted to disinfectant. The drones are out in force. The farm hands can't be far behind. I begin picking fruit myself. Once I've got an armload, I step out of the foliage.

The drones ignore me. I steady myself and breathe. In and out, feeling the chi of the land, sky, and somewhere, within me a river. In my right hand, a lemon. Fingers loosely encircle the waxy leathery ball, sense the weight of about 86 grams. It rolls around my upturned palm, finding the edges of my hand and recoiling back into the soft depression. Balance. I chuck it, not as hard as I can, not in desperation, with just the right amount of energy. It takes out the propeller on one corner of a drone about sixty feet away.

The thing lurches, drops a lemon. It can compensate to a degree, but only enough to return to base empty handed. It takes another direct hit and goes spinning wildly into the foliage. I swear I hear it scream. The other drones might be trying to let me have that one. Thinking that avoiding all out war might be their best option. That is, until I take out another one.

It flies low and close by, a payload of a perfect sour oblate spheroid dangling between it's landing gear. I swing my stick at it casually and turn it into a coaster with blinking lights. The other drones all turn to face me as I hold my staff aloft by the hilt in two hands, point down, and drive it like a stake through the heart of a vampire into this helpless automaton. It goes pop. The explosions of automobiles in movies from the seventies and eighties were much more dramatically satisfying, but I'll take a pop.

Slowly they all start moving towards my position, in a 360 degree net, closing in. I've got a pile of freshly picked produce at my feet and what amounts to a long sword as far as these sensitive little guys are concerned. Lemons fly in line drive pitches from my mound and drones are tilting, lilting, and crashing into one another. The closer they get to me, the more crowded the airspace. Just add lemons and the chaos is a little more than they can algorithmically process. Now the noises are a little more satisfying, as prop blades whinge into each other's vectors shearing each other to pieces in a wheee-shlackt-brrrvvvv. Lemons concussively landing on machine cowls and splitting the fine injection molded shells, thump-clack. Juice getting inside the breadboards, fizzht-jepeeeoorm-pop. Their language is fascinating.

They do close in on me one by one, but they really aren't armed with any kind of deterrent except invasion of personal space and bumping their props into me, which hurts them more than me. Eventually, I put

Lemons: In an Orchard

down the lemons and just start batting these guys out of the air. I have to duck a few times when the algorithm targets my head for a slam, but their angles of attack are all very predictable.

I send one about fifty feet into the air and it disintegrates into a shower of parts. A servo gear falling from the sky hits me in the eye. That's insulting. My cornea is covered in white lithium and the smear cripples my depth perception, so I drop the stick and just start throwing haymakers. I've destroyed the entire first wave of attack. There may not be a second, I'm not just going to wait around for them anyway. I head East, leaving behind me the most perplexing massacre of harmless technology for the field hands to puzzle over, if there are any people working on this farm.

The walk is arduous. My eye is tearing and stinging from the tiny impact and the grease. My foot squishes in my shoe like stepping on a week old pizza in its box. I don't think the ankle even hurts anymore, just feels really wrong. I'm wearing a girl's bedazzled denim jacket, shredded nylon joggers, and not much else. There are some spots on the jacket where the gemstones are missing, leaving blank shadows behind. Probably some of them were casualties to the drone attack. My neck is hot and red. My forehead, I can't see but I imagine is streaked like my leg with the various viscera I've been exposed to. I probably have the look of a backyard birthday clown dressed up as a Native American gone very very wrong. Like I drank a handle of vodka while getting dressed in a culturally insensitive gag costume to go to a party I wasn't invited to but aggressively pushed my way inside and did cartwheels around the back yard until I was tackled. At which point I'm sure in that fantasy I whipped out my genitals as a shield to put them on their heels. Then I'd make a speech about how they need to throw out the clutter in their lives and start naming the things around the yard which I can see that don't belong in an ordered and healthy environment for production. Starting with the happily married couple themselves, whom I observe have not held each other in protective embrace during my assault but have instead, taken up at opposite ends of the yard and attempted to prod me towards the other one, perhaps hoping for a psychotic miracle.

✱ ✱ ✱

Another memory comes to me. This one is a little further back in my young adulthood. I'm eighteen. Just graduating high school. I had my small group of friends. We've all begun working kind of regular, starter jobs. The kind that will use you six days a week and compensate you with fucking lollipops and free coffee. We were mingling with a slightly older crowd, girls who would eventually marry out of the grind they found themselves still bound to post-college. Good looking, hot young women with nothing to lose. One bedroom apartments where the rent was scraped together from tips and flirting, wondering what that poli-sci degree was good for after all.

It was also a bit of a party time for us. Having slightly older friends meant we aged in an accelerated fashion, were bestowed with the ability to purchase alcohol, which attracted other people, and other substances. I met Amy through some friends. She was always the center of attention in any room full of dicks. Not that she was a slut, or a tease, she was just a young woman, and men were men. I was not the picture of confidence that I have become. I wasn't very shy, but I didn't think I had a chance with her, until I did.

I remember drinking ourselves into a riot one night at her little apartment with the v-groove wood paneling and the kitchenette. I think her mother might have been visiting her, and she was a maniacal drinker who told stories all night and may have danced on the top of a two-seater breakfast-nook table, which would be a physics defying feat if it really happened.

I got so drunk that I went into the bathroom and sat on the toilet. I leaned just a little bit into a passing wave and blacked out momentarily, losing all muscle tone and folding forward and to the side striking my temple on the toilet paper holder. I came out of the bathroom thoroughly bloody and smiling like a geek. Her mom had gone to the bedroom and Amy was blowing up an air mattress in the living room. She said, have you ever had a foot massage?

I said, not yet.

She said, would you like one?

Yeah, I guess, sure. I laid down while she talked to me and pressed her delicate fingers like stones into the pressure points of my feet, and I went somewhere. This kind of affection between a man and a woman was new to me. It was not motherly, but it was intimate. She didn't know it, but she had gotten me too drunk to fuck and I was too remedial with girls to have even considered it, but as she worked her knuckles into my soles I drifted into a world where she would always be there and we would always be best friends. After I passed out, I don't know, but I imagine her curling up beside me and snuggling, probably having a hard time going to sleep. The bed deflated and we woke up on the floor. I had what might have been my first hangover. She made us breakfast, frozen Johnsonville sausage and some fried eggs. Breakfast never tasted so good.

A few weeks later at another party she came on stronger. And I responded. We were drunk by eight and around ten took a walk down from my cousins house to the motel at the end of the street where she worked as a desk clerk. She let us into the pool and we swam in our underwear. She came close, this half naked five foot one hundred pound coaxer of manhood. We were laughing about something when she came right into my bubble, put her arms around me and kissed my laughing mouth. I was stunned, but not for long. Her taste was nothing like I'd imagined. She had been smoking cigarettes and drinking beers, deeper base notes of her microbial and fungal biome blended with these top notes of party. Her saliva was soft and the inside of her mouth warm and small. Her teeth, which I licked the back of were smooth and clean.

Her small body wrapped tightly around mine under the edge of the pool lip, as we huddled together in a writhing breathy mess. Fingers and hands feeling each other's bodies. She felt my cock and her exhale went lower, much lower and ended in a groan in my ears which sounded so loud I thought I might have hearing damage

On the walk back to the party, the streetlights were holding their breath. A summer midnight wind blew up the street and she said, what if..

What if, I said.

Do you see those bushes right there? she said.

Those bushes? I said, pointing.

What do you think would happen if we went in there and had sex? It was the kind of drunk question only an eighteen year old me could have taken as anything other than sweet and shy. I worshiped her in a lot of ways. I wasn't listening to her really, my head was just buzzing from her sudden attack in the swimming pool.

I said, I wanna have sex with you Amy, but I value our friendship. Do you think we could still be friends after?

I don't know, she said. We were still walking. When we got back to the party. She went into a bedroom and lay down by herself. Looking back, twenty-two, her age was really young, especially for a girl who said, what do you think would happen if we had sex in those bushes, instead of fuck me over there, now. I had been given the invitation though, and I stood in that party a changed man. I drank everything that wasn't in someone's hand or mouth. In about ten minutes I found and guzzled all the alcohol left at the party. Then I went into that bedroom.

The next day, I called her and left a message. The day after that and so on. She wouldn't take my calls. I was heartbroken. There was this song I kept listening to over and over. It was a rock song about taking what we both wanted. The singer described breaking into a sleeping lovers house, eating her food and then slowly walking to the bedroom in the dark. It was transgressive and part of that element fit for me. Our whole thing had been a kind of tender transgression.

About a month later, it felt like years, she called. She wanted to take me out to dinner. We met at the local all night breakfast joint. The ceilings were low slung acoustical tiles drenched in grease. The place smelled like chili and armpits. We sat at the bar and she told me that we weren't going to be close friends anymore. Oh and yeah, she had met someone.

I didn't drink much after that party. Not at all. I never opened up that way to a woman again either. I turned my attention to my degree, my martial arts, my future as a late twentieth century minor robber baron. I didn't need that kind of pain in my life.

Lemons: In an Orchard

* * *

The trail opens up, and the sounds of a secondary highway take me by surprise. The resonant hum of rubber tires on pavement drills into my skull like the call of some lonesome animal. I fall down the embankment, sliding on my back. My jeep is still where I left it, in a turn-out. I reach under the fender for the key on top of the tire. The hand attached to my arm seems alien. It's covered in filth and cuts. It doesn't even seem to be the right age. The tendons are all knotted up and dehydrated. My fingers feel permanently clenched as I pull the key from it's shelter.

I open the passenger door. Something doesn't seem quite right, but I am exhausted. I sit down and take a big inhale and exhale. It smells like relief. My own smell, which is clean, permeates this space. I open the glove-box and pull out my phone. It is not dead, yet. Small miracle. I call Chet. It goes to voicemail.

Yeah, this is Chet, leave a message.

Hi, son. I'm out here in some lemon grove up past Bakersfield. I've been out in the elements for I don't know how long. I've been lost. I've been lost for a long time. I just found my way out though. Just got back to the Jeep, and I needed to tell you that, everything's gonna be okay, I...

Beep, if you are satisfied with your message, press one.

The interruption is comical. I press one.

To send your message with normal delivery, press one. To send your message with urgent notification, press two.

I press one. It isn't urgent anyway. The phone dies a few seconds later while I am taking a selfie of my disheveled face. My hands are shaking. I think I get a blurry shot of my rancid smile as the state trooper pulls up behind me. The screen goes unresponsive for a couple microseconds and then goes black. I look in the side view mirror and see the blue lights. I adjust the rear view and take a better look. Sunglasses, stony expression, stupid hat, yep, state trooper alright. I breathe a sigh of relief. I am rescued.

He walks up on the passenger side where I sit, in urgent need of medical assistance, and I suspect, counseling. Do you mind stepping out of the vehicle, sir? he says with perfunctory mechanism. His face is covered by a black paper surgical mask.

I can barely stand, officer, I say.

I'm a trooper, not an officer, he says. That was a strange distinction to be hung up on in this moment of crisis, but clearly he needs it.

Sorry, trooper, I say. My words came out funny. Trooooper. Sawree. I've just been lost in the grove for some days with no food.

Lemons: In an Orchard

I heard, he says. I feel a cold sensation in the middle of my spine. Now step out of the vehicle, he says.

I look into his eyes. They are not sympathetic. I say, I'd like you to call for an ambulance, trooper.. eh, what is your name?

Johnson, he says. His eyes flick to the right as he says it. You don't need an ambulance, he says. You look like Fuckles the Clown. I heard you and some other wetbacks were out here destroying drones, causing havoc.

Did he just call me wetback?

I lean my body, stick my leg out the open door, and place my hand on the arm rest. Leaning a little further on the right leg, which sears upwards with pain after sitting in a comfortable seat for fifteen minutes. My face shows pain. In fact it shows far more pain than I am actually in. So much pain that it draws officer Johnson to unconsciously stoop to give me support to get to my feet. Which throws him off balance, a position I leverage to turn him upside down rather quickly. He now lays on his back, with his head propped inside the Jeep against the edge of the seat. He reaches for his gun, I slam the door on his neck until it breaks, and then a few more times for good measure.

Exhausted and traumatized, I slump down in the dirt next to Johnson. His face is a retarded and bloody mess, face-mask slipped up onto his forehead looking like a rushed and doomed yarmulke. His leg still twitching. I lean and take his gun belt off. Once again, I am armed. I am still in the trap. There must be agents of the enemy everywhere out here. Perhaps the whole town is compromised. I think about the way my words sounded when I was speaking to Johnson, not my voice. I look back in my mind's eye to the moment I snapped my selfie, was that my face? In my memory, I can't be sure.

I press and pull myself into the seat again. rolling Johnson under the carriage of the vehicle to clear a path and make him look less suspicious. I turn the mirror and stare into Waldo's eyes. Donde esta Waldo, I whisper to my own transformed reflection.

I put the key in the ignition and turn it. Nothing. There had been none of the usual fanfare of bells and lights when I'd opened the door. Of course the battery is dead. A quick survey shows me that the hazards were left on. They would have blinked at a steady rhythm for a day, then they'd have slowed down imperceptibly at first, but geometrically toward the end. It would have been one of those cars on the side of the road that wink suddenly and weakly at unsuspecting drivers. Then, nothing. It probably died a week ago.

I rifle through Johnson's pockets. and find his keys. Limping over to the cruiser I become a spectacle to a pair of tourists in a motor-home who appear to slow, but then speed up as their better judgment takes control. His car has bio-metric ignition locks. It shuts itself off when I get in the driver's seat, and I imagine it also alerts the base. How can a shit little town like this afford this kind of tech? I have no tools and I have no time. I feel them closing in on me. There are no fancy locks on the shotgun or the trunk. So I take everything that I can carry in the way of armaments, which, with my leg the way it is, isn't much. But I find a first aid kit, a nice one, with a big old splint and tape and I gather that all up into a bundle I roll together with a bullet proof vest. I'm contemplating whether I have time to take Johnson's pants and whether they will fit me or not when I hear the chopper.

I drag myself back up the slope and hobble into the forest grid, my shredded pant-leg swirling in the wake of my flight. They haven't seen me yet, so I stay low and under bush. Crawling from tree to tree, I am invisible, but slow. Stopping to place the splint, I hear dogs barking at the roadside. Fuck me. I wish they were coyotes. The splint is tied off tight and the shotgun comes up just as the first K9 comes ripping into the foliage. They have no sense of danger. Trained to go balls out into conflict. They are not coyotes. There is a deafening blast and the head of a German Shepherd turns to pink mist in front of me. There are three more. My new shotgun is a seven round semi-automatic and three more shots shatter the idyllic Currier and Ives vibe as I snuff out the remainder of the scout regiment. Well, that's gonna piss them off. Certainly they had heard the blasts and would be holding off on rushing me again.

With the Kevlar vest in place and the gun slung under my chest, I crawl from tree to tree again while the chopper overhead, whirlybirds blindly unable to locate me with optics. My bedazzled denim jacket apparently is better camouflage than I would have imagined, that or the foliage is thicker.

I come to a place I feel like I recognize. Katrina is sitting under a tree. She is lovely and swollen and about to give birth. Her water has broken and the ground beneath her is a Rorschach ink blot of cervical fluid. She smiles when she sees me.

What did you do to me? I say, not able to whisper for my excitement and confusion and terror.

She looks calmly at me with a careful concern and says, everything is going to be alright. This is exactly as I was shown.

What the fuck are you talking about, I say, still unwilling to accept the magic I have been witnessing as anything other than the hallucinations of a dying man.

She says, come, hold my hands while I push.

I am dumbstruck. I know I can't fight off an armed regiment and a helicopter with just a shotgun and a flak jacket, and a part of me, my body, draws me to her instinctively. I crawl over to her where she leans with her back against the lemon tree. I take her hands in mine. The trees begin to change. The bright heavy fruit turns green and shrinks. The world is instantly without the sounds of the chopper and the chase. Instead the sound of a rewinding cassette of birds singing plays at a nearly subliminal volume. It's like stepping on a trapdoor just before the stage of a theater is engulfed in flames. I look to Katrina's eyes, they are the only thing around me not moving and shaking, vibrating. I don't know where she is taking us. Back to the village? I don't have room to care yet. The fight I have just been through in the world I came from is a final goodbye to anything that makes sense. At least in her world I know what has happened to my family.

*   *   *

I never thought, since my thirties, that I would be without money. In some timelines, namely the universe I took to be the only reality up until about a week ago, I have eighty million dollars stacked in the bank. When you have that kind of money, and you aren't a damn extravagant fool, it's enough to last you several lifetimes, or enough to buy your kids and kids lawyers a few things after you die. It kind of defined me in a way that was invisible to me.

I was such a successful guy. I felt like I had made all the right decisions to have earned what I did. Money is a state of mind. Turns out that much money has a gravity of its own. It pulls more money into itself, not just by accumulating interest. I could live off the interest of course, but in the sense that being a businessman with capital puts me in the position to act on a good deal when I see one. I can snap up a distressed business property for short cash money, which might be a million dollars! But the property is worth three, it just needs a house cleaning.

When you're at the level of flipping pre-war ranch homes, it's a grind. When you are at the level of turning around three and four story colonial era brick mixed use spaces in some of the most active markets in the country, you make money without even trying.

I met Lisa at a mixer for millionaires. When you are as successful as each of us was individually, the world and its people just look different. I wasn't gonna be into dating a waitress, or a barista, or a hairdresser. They were nice enough people sure, but they had money problems. Money attracts money. I wasn't there to be sugar daddy or solve anyone's problems. I wanted someone who had figured it out like I had, who had made her own way and was looking for an equal, a companion to share the good times with. To handle the vicissitudes of old age together with, someone who was done playing kids games.

Some friends introduced us at one of these things. I had seen her name around as she was a prominent local architect. She of course had never heard of me. I operate behind the veil of corporate interests, though I am far from a company man. We sat down at a little table at a posh exclusive restaurant I never would have gone to for any other reason on my own. The servers carried around trays of flutes sparkling with Moet, which was just what they were offering instead of ice water. I had a tap water. There were other trays on legs carrying a spectacle of hors d'oeuvres. An empanada drizzled with bright orange sauce sat on my small plate glaring up at me. It was kind of like art. Lisa had a glass of red wine and her delicate fingers commanded the stemware with poise, but her eyes were joking with me. She made light of how uninterested I looked at the fancy settings and food. I said, it's nice to be outdoors I guess. It was too. The summer air had cooled into the evening. I was wearing my typical outfit. I refused to dress up for these things. Cargo shorts and a t-shirt describing some charity event or another, and a black fleece with pockets I almost never used. People who keep their pockets full are a troubled lot.

We made it through the first half hour and were having a nice time. They brought us our meal. I had the chicken. She had the chicken. We talked about our families. She had lots of nieces and nephews. I had my two kids at that point. She had never been married, was a consummate business woman. She wasn't socially inept like me though, she had grace and people liked her. I liked her too. We exchanged cards.

The courtship was a lot of fun. We mostly did normal people stuff with rich person carefree attitudes. We ate at the decks. I almost never went out by myself, but she drew me out of my shell. We went to York's Wild Kingdom and she walked me through the petting zoo. I felt like I was at a conference with a bunch of touchy-feely entrepreneurs as goats swarmed us and bumped into our legs. She laughed at my face. Clearly you are in your element, she said.

I had to laugh too. I said, yehehehehehess. She burst into one of the biggest and most wholehearted laughs I had ever heard from a woman, at the end of which she snorted and covered her mouth, face turning red, body shaking from suppressing further outburst. We embraced there first, among the idiot goats and their kids. I wasn't into public displays of affection, but I couldn't help myself. I was in love. I kissed her, there while a goat ate through the pocket of my cargo shorts and ran off with the energy bar I had stashed there.

Now she was beyond my reach. Now, the money I had sitting in my accounts was going to be passed on to, who knew. How much of my family would be left to live their lives, and how long would the system stand as it was built? If the country, or even the world as it seemed, was on the brink of collapse, or revolution, how much would anything I had done to preserve myself and my family matter?

❋ ❋ ❋

I look down into Katrina's hands in mine. She pushes. I had been present for the births of most of my children. It's a point of pride for me. Be that what it is, it couldn't prepare me much for midwifing a teenage witch in a time-slip. I am not sure what I am supposed to do. She says, are you ready, doctor? What a sense of humor she has.

I say, kind of hard to time your contractions without my watch.

Lemons: In an Orchard

She says, that watch? between sharp breaths and points at my wrist, where, of course, Waldo's arm is wearing my watch. Then I have to face the fact that even with a watch, I didn't know where to start in timing her contractions when time itself is dilating around us. We seem to be hurtling backwards in time. The lemon trees are juveniles, then seedlings, then they disappear into the soil. The landscape turns to desert. Winds blow red earth back and forth. Day and night passes so quickly that the effect is faster than a strobe, more like the frames on an old television broadcast. The picture is almost seamless.

Katrina squeezes my hands with all her might, which is considerable and draws tears from my eyes, but I don't cry out. I know my threshold of physical pain well. What I have never advanced, is my threshold for emotional pain. I am coated in Teflon around other human beings, now something about humanity has reached inside me violently, and whether this is a dream or not, I feel for the first time that I am not alone.

Lisa had given me just a taste of this through her consistent affection for my sincere fumbling. But as much as I love her, she still shielded me from the world. If she hadn't, I wouldn't have fallen in love.

Now, Katrina, in a very vulnerable place herself, is showing me my own insignificance in the stream of time once again. I remember the lives of the other people I had seen before when I first fell into the river with Mani. How much they cared about things. How often they hurt and just kept going without putting up walls or executing power moves. How brave they were, and what a coward I am.

She pushes again. My knuckles crack in her grip. I look down beneath her skirt. It is soaked in liquid, kind of pink but not bloody. I can see her vagina opening. The pulsating power of those muscles as she gives birth. The child that is emerging, I can't see distinctly. I figure I am looking at the top of its head, but its body is a blinding light. She says, catch him.

Oh shit, really?

Really, she says.

I put my hands, backs down in the dirt beneath her knees and get ready. She gives a push and a holler so great that time shakes. The desert, which has gone through an ice age and become an ocean which we are at the bottom of, traversed by waves of ripples and bubbles which illuminate the cerulean matter like a glass kaleidoscope in the sun, and this infant, covered in viscous light, drops into my outstretched wetback palms. The world becomes as detailed as a mandala, all vision repeats and falls back upon itself, becomes reflection, dilates and drops again. Level after level of fractal crenelation travels on into infinity.

The time stream collapses, with us at the bottom of the primordial ocean vaporizing into a conscious mist, mixing with the tides of eternity.

11— HYDRATED WITH DOG VOMIT

I **blink my eyes. My back is supported by a soft covering on a hard surface.**

My fingers reach out and feel. Grass. The sky above me is solid turquoise. In one corner of my vision, a bright light coming from a yellow ball. Something licks my cheek. I'm stunned so at first it has free reign on my face for at least five solid licks before I'm able to raise my arms and shoo it away. Damn dog. The boy laughs at me. I sit up. My back is on fire, as though I'd laid here with a rock in my pocket for a week. I reach into my pocket, pull out my watch. It is broken. I look at the boy. He just looks me in the eye and shrugs. Kids.

I look around. We are sitting on the bank of the river. The trees nearby are in blossom still, though decidedly fewer flowers. I sniff the air. The smell is of endless spring on the verge of crashing into unyielding summer.

The boy says, welcome back retard. The dog whines. She was worried about you, he says.

Well, Puedes, you didn't let her sleep with me did you?

She wouldn't leave your side, he says. She brought you water while you slept. I held you up and she drank from the river and spit it in your mouth. You drank it. Your body wanted to live.

Gross, I say. I've been hydrated with dog vomit?

I guess, he says.

Where is everyone else? Why didn't they move me inside and cover me with a blanket or something?

That's not how it works. If we moved your body, your spirit wouldn't have been able to find it when it returned from the journey, he says.

I just look at him. My face I'm sure is stuck in a kind of dumbstruck impotent aggravation. That's what it feels like. Noticing this, I soften the edges of my eyes and let my mouth go slack. It feels better that way. What the hell is happening to me? I ask the boy.

Well, a couple of years ago, one of the people of our village experienced exploding in rainbows. Was it like that? he says, his tone so nonchalant, I am sure he is fucking with me.

No, It was like a hologram though.

Lights?

Well, yeah. But, I, we were inside them and they were like a sculpture that was alive. I don't know how to describe it, Puedes. That's not really my thing.

So, you saw the projection of consciousness at the beginning of time?

I shoulda taken a picture, then I could just show you.

You can't take a picture in the spirit realm, he said, as if I didn't know that. I made a retard face at him.

Do you know what a kaleidoscope is? I say.

Yeah.

How do you know what a kaleidoscope is?

The beekeeper has one, and I can see it in your mind.

Why don't you just look in my mind and see the thing I saw then?

Because it's better if you tell me that sort of thing.

Well, it was a baby, made out of a kaleidoscope.

Yeah, you saw the rainbow explosion thing, he said.

This whole time he's been finding rocks in the grass and throwing them over his shoulder into the river. The dog watching him looks puzzled. Damned dog and its facial expressions.

Do you want to see Chet again?

Last time it didn't go very well, I say.

Yeah, but, he says.

I know, I say. Lead the way, Puedes.

Okay retard, he says with so much compassion in his voice I have to laugh. He gives me a dirty look. The dog looks back and forth between us. Her face inscrutable for once. He leads me through the grove. Its trees look ancient and thick. The flowers tremble in the sunshine, white five pointed stars constellating in a galaxy map. Each one a sun home to multiple planets. Each one sending out waves of sweet aromatic cologne. I smell something else over the blossoms. It pricks my nose up and makes me look around.

I see the old man sitting in his wicker chair, smoking a pipe. The smoke curls out and hangs low, drifting across the grove. Bees are swarming in the wake and flying through it taking big gulps, growing lazy and content from the haze. He sees us and lifts his pipe in salute. Who is that? I ask the boy.

That is the beekeeper, he says as if it should have been obvious.

I met him before I came here, I say. He doesn't respond to me, but waves at the old man. His determination to get us back to the village swiftly shows in his gait. We do not slow down or take a detour to see the man, and after my first interaction with him, I'm glad. He tricked me into eating coyote guts, I say. The dog looks at me and whines.

Lemons: In an Orchard

You tricked yourself, retard. He only tried to help you. He may seem wise, but he doesn't understand everything. He understands bees real good, and portals. He's really good with portals.

Portals? I ask.

Don't ask stupid questions, he says, staring straight ahead into the long straight path. He's the only other person besides you who talks about the rainbow explosion. We walk for about an hour before coming back to the village outskirts where we find the saddest looking little hut has been transformed. The sunlight is on it, it looks warm. The boy shouts through the door. Once again the old man inside calls for us to come in.

He is sitting in one of those lemon branch shaker chairs. His table is also a tree trunk. He's smiling, not like a madman or a fanatic, just kind of peaceful. I remember last time he hadn't been so pleasant looking, nor had he been able to get out of bed. Not dead yet? I ask, before considering my words too carefully.

No, I'm quite well today. The girls just brought me some lemon tea with honey, he says.

Look, about last time.

You wanna touch my pecker still?

That's not funny.

It is to an old man. Look, I know what you're gonna say.

No you don't, that's ridiculous. I just wanted to say I'm sorry.

I knew it.

Sure, you did.

I'm sorry too, he says. I'm sorry for the way I treated you last time. It was very emotional for me, and at my age, emotions are extra strong. I don't hate you. The man who came out here fifty years ago hated the man who set foot in that lemon grove two weeks ago, but neither one of us is either of those people anymore. I've had fifty years to forgive you, and I balked at the first opportunity.

Forgive me?

Yeah, dad, that's funny, an old fucker like me calling a young man like you dad. Dad, you were a terrible father. Most men of our time were though. And I can see you've changed. Whether that's an effect of my troubled eyesight or a fact, doesn't really matter at this moment. Do you know why?

I guess fifty years goes by and you don't really worry about the same things you used to, I say, fumbling.

More or less, but the answer I was thinking is that I've changed. When I came here I was a boy of nearly thirty. I was desperate for something I could never have and without realizing it I was depriving myself of everything that I did have. I wanted your approval dad.

But you had it, the whole time, I love you so much.

No, the fact is, you can't give it to me. I want it from the version of you that lives inside my head, for the version of me that lives inside my head.

Lemons: In an Orchard

I think fifty years in a lemon grove has given you some kind of way of saying things.

Probably. The point is, I'm glad you're here. I'm glad you came.

I'm glad I'm here too, Chet. I can feel tears weeping down my cheeks.

He says, don't cry pussy. Then he stands up, walks toward me and embraces me. We both cry. The boy and the dog look at each other and roll eyes. Now, he says, I'm old and my bowel movements are infrequent. I feel one coming and I'm not about to ignore the signs. I did that a few weeks ago and spent an hour in the river afterwards. I was pretty sure I'd come out reborn as a Jesus lizard or some kind of iguana, but I was returned to my body, just a little cleaner.

Yeah, that river.

Yeah, get out. I'll see you later, dad. He shoes us out the door and totters off down the path to the latrine with his hand over his rear end. I look at the boy. He is smiling.

Better? he asks.

I'd like to see Abuela.

You mean Katrina?

Sure, I say.

He motions and I follow him. The dog stays at my side and when I look down at her she pushes her wet nose into my hand until I scratch her behind the ears. She does this several times. We walk past jars of lemons, juice in various stages of processes that will turn it into liquor, cleaning fluid, lemon oil for lanterns and medicinal use. There are stacks of lemon cookies fresh from an earthen oven cooling under the shade of an awning. There are jars of lemon rinds preserved like candy.

* * *

Katrina meets us at the door and ushers us inside. She has a fresh pot of tea waiting for us. We sit around her table and sip tea and eat biscuits. We talk about the history of the grove, how it goes back far further than the miracle of the village. Thousands of years ago this grove was the home to a people who knew how to heal all human ills and could travel to the stars with their minds. When the Spanish colonials came, it was obvious to the star people, the portent of war to come that would be wrought across the earth like an iron cage. They recognized the limits of their own powers. They saw the face of the human ills there was no cure for, greed, anger, blood-lust, power. The elders got together and in the largest ceremony they had ever performed, they cast seven spells.

The first one blessed the soil. This dirt will always be fertile ground, not just for trees, but for spiritual growth.

The second spell blessed the rains, that even though infrequently falling from the sky, the river would always come down the mountain, even in the driest weather.

Lemons: In an Orchard

The third spell blessed travelers through this land, that they would be safe and find things here in themselves that they didn't know about, like strength and courage. Not the courage to do battle, but the courage to make peace.

The fourth spell was to make this place a spiritual crossroads. Many people here are not what they seem. There are spirits of long dead folk, interstellar travelers, and minor deities walking the paths in harmony with the descendants of the first post-world group. This place is a portal hub.

The fifth spell told the coyotes they were to evolve and to become useful to the people who traveled here. They were not to be a menace. I took minor issue with this spell but, I digressed after the dog looked at me and whined.

The sixth spell was that of a general blessing for the planet. With the seventh, they all completely disappeared. Traveled somewhere no conquistador nor European after them could follow. They left behind artifacts, but no written history. The story of these people was passed down by the few who stayed behind to care-take the planet and the sacred portal land. Should a time come in the future when it was safe to return, they thought they might. These descendants lived among the American Indian tribes for hundreds more years, many were killed alongside their new tribesmen in the slaughters that followed the initial colonization, but a few survived. They carried their history with them and passed it on like a weight to their children, most of whom are here in this village today. They have rejoined the magic of their ancestors, who will never return, now they are sure of that.

I listen with rapt attention like I never have listened to a story before. The boy even jokes that I act now more like a child than him. Katrina then asks me, who do you think blew up the world outside?

I guess it was probably the government doing some fool thing in conflict over some resource, I say. Perhaps some artificial intelligence took over and bombed the shit out of us. Maybe it was aliens, came and wiped us out to take our resources. I haven't even heard what it looks like out there. No one will really tell me anything. Is it a wasteland? It is all grown over with weeds and brush? Are there grizzly bears roaming the streets of downtown Manhattan?

This land is blessed, remember. The rest of the planet, none of us has seen it in person. Sometimes it is visible to us in astral projection. It is doing much better without us. So we've decided to leave it that way.

It wasn't the government, she says. Not the drones or the machines. Not a lone madman or an environmental coup. We all did it in one way or another. It was that we believed we deserved retribution. All the atrocity, the wars, disease, and the eventual collapse of civilization into a bleeding screaming nightmare, was because we wanted it to happen. Nothing could have held us back. When eight billion people decide that things aren't okay all at once, and everyone gets an idea of how to make their little section of the planet okay for them, it's not war.

It's anarchy, I say.

No, anarchy is reality. Even selfishness can be used for good or harm. Fear is what leads to the mice eating the shoes.

Not this again, I say.

They won't eat your shoes anymore dear. You've seen the inside. It may take a little while for you to grow into it, but you will. I think your son will be a big help.

Chet does seem to be warming up to me.

My heart breaks for your love, but I'm not talking about that son, she says. I'm talking about Mani.

Who? I ask. The boy kicks me and points at his chest with his thumb.

Me, retard, he says.

I look at him. His face had become so familiar I had not recognized him when he was born at the bottom of the ocean, all glowing rainbows. Hadn't seen that the collapse of the time stream came upon the birth of his twin sister, the dog, as her infant howl had toppled the bubble of finite structure that had surrounded us. Oh, Puedes, I say.

12— A DANGLING SWORD

After tea, I declare that I need my space for reflection.

I've been lost in a lemon grove by myself, now somehow surrounded by more people than I know what to do with.

I have found a family and they weren't letting me go anywhere. If they were to be believed, there is nowhere to go. I mean, it is highly unlikely that these hundred or so people represented the last of mankind, there are probably pockets like this all over the place, but they aren't doing trade, they aren't having mixers and exchanging DNA. Life has gone tribal in a pre-traditional sense. People aren't ready to come out from hiding so-to-speak. Whatever it was that had killed so many of us fifty years ago had left an impression, such that they don't want to talk about it, and they don't want to move on from it back into a retaking of the Earth. I'm in no position to demand answers. It is my frustration, but it is nobody's fault. Something has happened here, long before I came along, that made this place what it is. I just happened to stumble into it at the exact moment whatever spirit was waking up from however long a slumber. I can't believe it, but I can accept it. It seems that fighting it is exhausting and impossible. I am along for the ride now.

The sun has gone down and murmuring people are everywhere preparing their meals, caring for each other with such a level of attentiveness I have only seen in documentaries. Even in those films what I saw was the process of care, the function of the whole as a method for improving efficiency. What I observe here I feel differently about. Weaving in between the huts, my hands in the pockets of the overalls I'd gaffled from some workers bench, I feel a distinct lack of pressure. The villagers see me walking, I catch their eyes and even in the fading light of dusk I can see their faces soften and warm as though each of us were a fire that warms the other. I see it and feel it in my own face responding to theirs.

Children by the multitudes swarm around the adults. Their childhood imaginations create a thickness of the atmosphere at three feet elevation above the ground. Their bodies seem capable of flight within this narrow band, and their curiosity so boundless that it expands the compressed space of childhood from within that three feet to the breadth of an entire sky. I watch as the adults in this world seem aware of the creative limitlessness of the minds of their offspring and nurture it.

I wince as I remember making sand castles with Chet. I was the project manager, he was the foreman. Every time his imagination wanted to place a dragon shaped pillar beneath a corner of a tower, I had explained why such things were impossible with sand. Especially if we wanted to have a good foundation. Look at the pyramids of Egypt, you don't see any dragon statues under those I said. I remembered how crushed he looked in that moment, and how quickly he worked past it and became my little soldier for the rational army.

The path winds itself through the village casually. It never goes anywhere in a hurry. As I walk on I come to the edge of the development. The backs of the huts are all painted with a camouflage of sorts, covered in stylized lemon flowers. The paint is layers thick, It seemed that they repaint it every season to reflect the changes and growth. It has a funny look to it. It isn't exactly paint. Some assortment of pigments derived from what I know not. The white of the flowers is a kind of powder adhered with... I lean in and smell the wall. Honey. The paint is made of honey. The flowers on the wall smell sweet. I imagine in summer time, lemons will also come to be painted here.

Turning back out of the village, I stroll toward the mountains which loom in the distance. I think about my bank account. If I could weigh the relative security of having eighty million dollars in the bank against what I found here in this village, I have to admit that money couldn't buy this peace. I have to admit how useless that money is, even when I had access to it and a world to spend it in. I'd spent my whole life being a sycophant for money. This is the gentle punchline. For all my coaxing of variables, my private Hawthorne experiments, in manipulating the world around me, I had manipulated myself. Oh well, it was spilt milk. I am here now, and despite my greatest attempts, things are alright.

There is something below the horizon. In the moonlight, there are grasses creeping higher toward the foothills. They sway in lunar gray-scale against the indigo sky. Something Lucifer black amidst them does not move. It watches me silently. My feet are directed to it by some pedestrian curiosity. As I get closer the shape becomes clearer and I can make out why it isn't moving. It's a cave entrance. A feeling creeps into my skin as I notice how similar it is to one of my fevered dreams atop a lemon tree. The sense that everything has led me here is an ominous reflection. I should go back to the village and get a torch. I should ask someone about this cave.

I stand there, fifty feet from the gaping maw of the underworld, staring into the abyss. I don't know how long. I have not eaten dinner and my stomach rumbles. My weight shifts back and forth on my feet. I feel something under the toe of my right foot. Thinking it is a rock, I scrape at it with the sole of my shoe. It makes a funny noise, a steel ringing sound. Scooping the thing up, I know instantly it is a Zippo lighter. Is this where all the pens and lighters and socks end up? Is that the eighth blessing bestowed upon the earth and this grove by the ancient ones? I flick the cap open and sniff it. It is loaded with some kind of distilled lemon oil rocket fuel. The smell is so potent it almost knocks me over. When I spin the wheel, a gush of sparks shoot out and a flame the size of a crayon flares up.

I flick it shut again and walk toward the cave. At the entrance I stop and listen with my ear leaned into the black hole. It has the shape of a mouth with the corners turned down. Six feet tall at the center. I flick on the lighter. The illumination reveals a torchiere held to the wall like a primitive sconce. I hold the lighter to it and it bursts into a fiery bloom. Blue flames lick up to the top of the oil soaked fabric and warm into a bright orange ball. I pick it from its bracket, a convenient notch in the rock of the cave, and I walk inside.

Lemons: In an Orchard

The path inside leads down sharply. I think I might slip and tumble so I go slow and gentle, taking each step with immaculate care. I am probably a hundred feet deep when the tunnel opens up into a large room. I am in a great antechamber. The walls are lined with movie posters in darkened frames. The ceiling appears to be a skyward reaching dome, with a glass chandelier hanging too low, stretched to the limits of the wiring supporting its full weight, as it had been dislodged from a mounting hook by some catastrophe or another. I imagine what that looked like.

This room was a well lit carnival of citizens distracted by their own narratives, here on a first date, or to reconcile a failing marriage going on a date night as suggested by their therapist, every one of them thinking about their own shit. None of them foreseeing a cataclysm that would rock their concepts of a free life to the core.

Then I see it happen. In movies people scream during an earthquake. In my fantasy, everyone is too shocked to scream, they just drop to their knees and start crawling. Their faces turn to a depth of fear surpassing anguish. Many of them begin to cry. Some of them are looking up as this massive chandelier starts to plummet. There is a young couple huddled beneath it. They are holding each other by the shoulders and their cheeks are touching as they mumble their end of the world prayers into each other's ears. They don't know it, but their love is the most pure on the planet in that moment. The fact that they are not going to die alone prompts the fates to hold off and try to get them at a later date, when they will be separated by another circumstance. The wiring of the big lamp is snapped taut like a whip. It makes a cracking noise as the weight of the thing is transferred up the line to the ceiling box, where some handfuls of dust and debris are shaken loose by the massive seismic activity of the ground and the pull of the weight of a five hundred pound light fixture stopped just a mere six feet from the floor.

The couple hear the noise. The woman wets her pants. But they are alive. They crawl out from under that dangling Sword of Damocles and run for better cover, arm in arm. Nobody is screaming.

I walk to a concession counter. Collapsed glass and steel cases long ago emptied of treats either by hungry survivors or rats. Tracing along the counter with my torch, a breeze pulls the flame. I shudder to wonder if I am alone down here now. The flame has pointed up the line, toward the ticket check. The carpet beneath my feet covered in dust. There are no other footprints, which is comforting.

Into the back of the house I go. The trail is littered with five decade old theater garbage. The silence is deep. I open the double doors to one theater and am greeted by a wall of debris packed solid. There are probably a hundred mummified corpses in there. I shut the doors and walk on until a breeze pulls me into a set of doors. The theater inside is undamaged. The curtains still hang on the walls, twenty-five feet up in the dark, the red velvet crenelations against the wall are still. My eyes play tricks though and I think I see movement. With the light from the torch being one big flicker, it must be an artifact of the lighting. There is no sound. Nothing is moving down here.

The aisle is littered with rat shit and an inch of dust. The screen is smooth and silent. The slope of the house pulls me toward the screen and to the exit doors at the bottom. The exit signs are in retirement. Their back up batteries might have lasted a year at the most once the power was cut off, presumably by a hundred feet of earth being dumped over everything.

Standing at the base of the screen, I once again see movement in the corner of my eye, high up in the catwalk, but the light won't stay still long enough for me to get a good look. I put my hand on the crash bar of the door. A noise like a door slamming hard from somewhere else in the theater strikes at my core. I feel my insides turn to jelly. With as much stealth as I can manage with my balls in my throat I push on the crash bar. The door is blocked on the other side. I look across the foot of the stage at the other door and move towards it. Again sensing movement above me which now feels sinister. The hairs on the back of my neck point straight at the sky and my adrenaline spikes. I hit the other crash bar with considerably less stealth than before and burst through it. There is no obstruction, but there is plenty of debris. I look back into the theater, and by the light of the torch I swear I see something fall from the ceiling and hit the ground silently. The door slams shut on this unseen horror and I find a brace on the ground and shove it in place against the door.

Within seconds something from the other side hits the crash bar and drives my brace six inches into the asphalt. I slam it shut again and place more debris in the path. It hits again and scatters much of the garbage out of the alley and into the street beyond. I decide to make a run for it, my torch is now streaming flames back behind me, pointing in horror at whatever is leaning heavily into that door. I'm so panicked that I run for some number of blocks before I realize I'm running through a living city. There are electric lights on in some of the windows. The streets are lined with dead cars, all pieced and parted out until just the assembly line looking carriages are left, almost feather-light-looking, nowhere left to go, picked clean like the desert bones of prairie cattle.

13— THE MICE WILL EAT YOUR SHOES!

I stop running. The streetlights are bright enough that I feel silly carrying a torch.

How does one douse a torch though. I don't want to just leave it burning, but as I look around the method escapes me for extinguishing this thing. I blow on it and it glows brighter. I try to roll it on the ground and it still glows brighter. In the end I find what might have been a

Volkswagen and stick the handle end of the torch into the hole meant for the top of the strut, which has long ago been confiscated perhaps to put a suspension on some underground dweller's donkey cart.

I smack my hands together and look around some. The buildings are urban, brick and concrete. The skies are phosphor gray. Towering four and five stories above me and all around me are the remnants of the suburban architectural foothills of an outer belt business district of some sort. I try to gauge by the sky how far this cavern looms beneath the grove and the river, but I cannot. It doesn't seem to end, which I assume to be some sort of visual hallucination.

Silhouettes move behind shaded glass lit from amber rooms beyond. These nondescript lives behind screens, they seem routine enough, as though no one were worried about the monsters in the movie theater. How can they possibly not know about that thing? They're in these apartments living like the world hasn't ended. I lean into one of the windows, which is closed, and try to listen through the glass to what conversation might be happening on the other side, but I get nothing. Strangely, the occupant shadows seem to notice me and they freeze in place, then they disappear. Maybe they aren't as comfortable as they seem.

I listen to the street. Breezes blow and topple empty bottles in the alley to my right. Then voices are carried up out of that same alley. I walk cautiously between the two buildings, straining my eyes into the bleak darkness before me. I see a light flicker briefly and make a noise like all the air being sucked out of a bottle, Phoomp!

I stop dead in my tracks to contemplate the will-o-the-wisp that just revealed itself at the back of the alley. The mice ate his shoes. I hear a voice say.

Great, these mice are everywhere, I mutter. Moving forward into the circle where the alley opens up into a sort of courtyard, there is a metal drum cut in half, filled with phosphorescent crystals giving off some heat and light. A ring of hobos surrounds it. They are drinking hooch from unlabeled glass bottles. I approach, but they don't take much notice. Either I'm boring or I'm an apparition from one of the bottles and not to be trusted or assumed to be extant in any degree. I try to open a conversation by saying, have any of you guys been to the movies lately?

They sit in relative quiet, ignoring my question. I think I'm not going to get any answer until one of them turns and looks at me. Finishing his appraisal he says, oh, it's you. Yeah, I went just last night, saw A Nightmare on Grove St part twelve. I can't tell if he is pulling my chain or not.

I say, is that the one where you end up in an underground movie theater and get chased by a ceiling dweller into a black sky city?

That sounds about right, he says. What do you want? he asks as he holds an empty bottle up in the light of the crystal fire and strikes a match, dipping the tip into the mouth of the bottle, creating a plume of flame shooting out and a wall of blue fire crawling in, while the noise resounds, a hollow vacuum suction. It sounds like a man getting the wind knocked out of him.

I don't know, I say. I had more money than I could ever spend. I suppose that's still waiting for me somewhere.

What good is money you can't spend? asks another one of the vagrants. I can smell his breath turning to acid across the fire. The flames turn green momentarily, then flicker back to a bright black glow.

I don't know, I say again. What's the point of all this then? Trying to scare me?

What makes you think you are important enough to be the center of attention here? You think everything is designed personally with you in mind? To either please or terrify you?

I look at him. At this point I am used to getting no respect from anyone who I encounter on my journey.

What you saw in the theater, he says, what do you think it was?

I don't know. I was hoping you'd tell me, I say.

What makes you think we know? he says. This place is feeling more unfriendly than I had hoped. Lightning flashes across the fluorescent gray sky. It lights the faces of the men at the can fire. They are all board members from my former company. I can't remember their names. They have never been that important to me.

Wanna drink? asks another one. He holds out a bottle of yellow liquid with an animal fetus growing in it.

I gag. They all laugh horrendously. Fine, I say. I take the bottle. They look at me incredulously now. I tip it to my lips, all the while my eyes watching them around the edges of the bottle as they anticipate my reaction. The liquor touches my lips. It produces a warmth in my face greater than that of the phosphorescent flames. It tastes vaguely of mushrooms and smells of piss. I take a long guzzle. The fetus in the bottle is moving, alive. I try to discern what animal it is that would grow in ether. Look at its two arms and two legs, its tail, its head, and decide it had to be something like a man, though clearly not entirely.

Welcome to the board, says the first man, his face a sunken wreck. His clothes a shabby version of a cheap suit left out in the weather on a plaster dummy which begins to melt and seep white mud into the weave. His companions cheer in report. My head feels like an expanding balloon, the skin of my face stretched tight across a burgeoning skull. I hand the bottle back and they pass it around and empty it. Then the last man to guzzle lights a match and makes the ghost jump in the bottle again.

How long have you guys been down here? I say. They don't appear to have aged fifty years like everyone I met topside. In fact, they look rather well preserved.

The Mice Will Eat Your Shoes!

Mice ate our shoes. Time stopped on that day. We have no more records, are three responses they utter in order by three different respondents.

I look down at their feet. They are wearing shoes. I say, if the mice ate your shoes, where'd you get those?

Target, up the road, says one man and he laughs so hard he chokes, coughs, and spits into the crystals which sizzle and steam. A hiss rises from the circle. He has a face like a jaundiced beach ball, his five o clock shadow tearing pill out of his oxford collar.

I think I see movement on the brick walls above and look up. In the shadows, there is no stillness. the dark seems to swarm and squirm beneath the radiant glow of the cavern roof. I say, do these things bother you? and point up.

We don't look up, says another man. His eyes in fact not leaving the ground in front of him as if to demonstrate his commitment to the idea.

I feel something lick the back of my neck and I jump.

Have another swiggle, says the man and hands me another bottle without looking up. I take it in my hand and this time the embryonic tenant looks me in the eye and winks. I toss back the whole thing and watch the circle gape in awe at my chutzpah. I feel the little homunculus swim down my throat with the stream. He takes up residence in my belly and begins giving lessons to the digestive system on how to play a marching song entirely on an orchestra of tubas.

Lemons: In an Orchard

I toss the bottle to one of the men. It hits him square between the eyes and he falls forward with his hands over his face, blood trickling out from between his fingers. Owww, he moans and rocks back and forth. The others look around nervously from side to side. Shoulda looked up, I say. No one laughs. The bottle rolls on the ground in front of his feet. The man next to him picks it up and completes the ritual of releasing the spirit. I feel the homunculus in my gut squirm and die as if his soul has just been torched.

Well, I say, you guys have been no help at all.

Cheers, they all ring out except for the one I damaged with the bottle. He just looks at me with one burning eye from between his fingers pressed to his face. His gaze is hurt and angry and I think for a moment he might get up and stab at me with a shattered bottle in his grip like some avenging drunken master. Then he utters, far out of sync with the others, cheers, in a small croaking voice, as though he were going to cry about it.

I look behind the group and see a door. Where does that door go? I ask.

They all turn, except the hurt man, and look at the door. One of them with a large pimple on the end of his nose says, that door goes inside that building. That building is not a great place to be, but it beats the movie theater. This elicits cacophonous laughter from the group. The hurt man mutters something.

I ask, what?

The Mice Will Eat Your Shoes!

He looks up, tears his hands from his face, all pale and streaked with dark blood, screams, the mice will eat your fucking shoes man! Then goes back to contemplating his inner palms.

I walk around the group. My feet kicking bottles out of the way. They go ringing off into the dark corners where something slides down the wall and slurps them up with a tongue the size of a wacky noodle. I feel the wet spot on the back of my neck. It is warm and slick. The door pulls open and a hallway stretches out in front of me, lit by a string of construction lights and full of boxes of paperwork covered in dust. Some kind of archive. The door shuts behind me while the circle of jerks is laughing uproariously about another joke, and the hurt man glares in my direction with one eye from between his fingers.

* * *

I lean against the wall for a moment, my head spins lightly, like a big windmill turning very slowly on a still day. I feel my vision has to be constantly adjusted by a half a degree change every six seconds or so or I'll simply tip over and wind up with my head stuffed in one of these boxes.

While I'm leaning I flick a cardboard lid off one of the boxes and rifle through the folders inside. It's all numbers. There isn't a single letter in any language. All numbers arranged in paragraphs and sentences, headings, file labels. Even the suggestion of a photograph is done with numerals arranged so that the gestalt pattern forms a picture, and that picture is of the numeral seven.

I have been hoping for something useful. Instead, I feel violated. I pick up the cardboard banker's box in the heft of my arms and throw it into the hallway. It hits the ground and comes apart, stacks of sheets of paper covered in meaningless numbers cascade across the cement floor like spilled liquid, stopping when the surface tension of the meniscus overcomes the momentum of the puddle. A light above my head, bare bulb hanging almost in my path, flickers. I turn it with my fingers first to tight, which does nothing, then to the left to loosen and to turn it off altogether. There are plenty of lights in the ceiling, I don't need that one.

I step over the exploded wreck of the box and onto the paper-slide. My sneakers leave peculiar tread marks on the paper. As I look back, I think, those look different. I kneel down and take a closer look. Each print is comprised of hundreds of smaller prints like those of a rodent, over-layed, tessellated, they seem to connect numbers to other numbers in an organic equation. I still can't read it, not having studied the STEM schools as much as business management and totalitarian ethics, etc.

The pit of my stomach is bottomless now. I have ventured out to clear my head and been sucked instead into deeper mystery. I have been up all night with recourse for rest. There is nothing comfortable about this dungeon world. I can not be compelled to close my eyes for more than a blink, and sometimes winking through a wave of fatigue, I will only close one at a time, lest something get the drop on me.

Now I look at the soles of my shoes for clues. They look like I remembered, which is not in any sense a clarification of what I was seeing on the paper.

I look over my shoulder at the hallway stretching out before me. My neck cracks. I feel like it is headed down, imperceptibly creeping into the core of the planet. I stand up and feel a creaking in my knees, I sway a little. Hungry, probably. Tired, definitely. The path ahead of me draws me onward. Lined all the way with these stupid inscrutable bank boxes full of what feels like one impossibly long number, separated by commas every third digit. Lights that flicker when I get near, so eventually I give up trying to reset them. They are reacting to my presence, not the other way around. This place knows I am here. It wants me to know that it knows. I am uncertain how I feel about that. Looking over my shoulder repeatedly as I walk becomes a burden as it only increases the probability in my mind that something will be there when I turn around. So I keep my head and eyes focused ahead of me. After doing this for a few minutes I become aware of my ears. They are playing jingles in my head. Maxwell house coffee, brown eggs, General's auto insurance, Allen Wayside Furniture. I feel the prick of whispers over inhuman tongues creeping out from the long dark behind me.

Looking is not going to help, I decide. Until the maddening sounds become overwhelming, I will not turn around. There is nothing there, so I tell myself that what I am hearing is the natural progression of a hallucination that had begun to form in my visual cortex being transferred to my auditory centers. The world is always singing and I am in my hyper-vigilant state just now more aware of the changes in the tempo, volume, and melody of that song. My own footsteps leave a flat slapping sound on the concrete and do not reverberate due to the presence of so much baffling material. I walk at a good clip for an old guy with a healing leg. Time stretches and loses meaning in such a space. I feel I have been walking for hours when I come to another door. Has it been hours, or has it been fifteen minutes?

I stop in front of this new gray steel rectangle. I listen to the manic sounds in my head turn their echolocation onto establishing a pattern for what might be on the other side. I squeeze my eyes shut, put my hand, palm out, on the metal door. It rumbles with the force of life. This could be my last chance of exit for a while. If I keep walking I might come to another door I might not see one for days. I listen hard, but hear little. I try to look in the cracks around the door, either it is completely dark on the other side or they are sealed up too tight for me to see any light. Then I noticed the keyhole is ancient, probably two hundred years old, and that means it will also work as an observation porthole.

Once again kneeling I slowly position my eye in line with it from about three feet back, just in case. I can see light. I can see faint movement as well. I am drawn closer to the hole. Each second that I am not met with a skewer being poked out at me I advance another inch. The picture is not much clearer until I am within six inches of the hole. It begins to change from a swirling mess of motion and gray-scale pixelation into a writhing mass of furry bodies. I am sucked all the way up to the hole, nearly scratching my cornea on the machined opening. There is another hallway, intersecting this one. It stretches to a similar infinite length. Floor and walls and ceiling are covered with white, gray, and black mice. They squirm and claw and now I can hear it, they squeak and squeal. I feel a shiver up my spine and through the edges of my vision see a corresponding flicker in the bulb above my head.

In my crouched position my body succumbs to fatigue momentarily. I feel a weakness, a gray-out passes over me and I lose some control of my balance. I lean suddenly and hard into the door. It punches the door frame and rebounds. This is when I notice something else about this door. The latch bolt is missing from the lock-set. When I recover from my spell, I realize that the door is not and can not be shut.

The mice take note of my presence and scramble out of the opening and into the hallway with me. They run up my pant legs and under my shirt, biting me ferociously. They nibble at the soles of my shoes as I stomp about, shaking and jarring my body to send shock-waves through my flesh to dislodge the tiny predators. Then, I run.

My heart is in good shape. My joints are frequently stress tested at the gym. I live an active lifestyle. I usually run in my neighborhood or on a track at my gym. This tunnel is nothing like the controlled environment of that track, but spurred by the horde of angry mice at my heels I dodge low hanging pipes and light bulbs and hip check boxes into the path behind me, hoping to slow them down. They are a flood, a wave of thinking molecules bent on the task of tearing me to pieces bite by tiny bite. Why oh why had this not been some sick inside joke when I'd heard it. I had no idea this was a literal hazard.

Having been a runner in a highly controlled environment gives me a great deal of knowledge about my body, enabling me to time with certainty, what would otherwise be an indefinable space. I am well aware of the pre-quarter mile shin splints and ankle creases that are calling for my system to produce and deliver the cortisone shots to those extremities which are experiencing duress. I am also prepared for the three quarter mile drop in blood sugar that precipitates the feeling of hopelessness that always gives me the inevitable irrational fear that I am wasting my time and I should just quit. At two miles, I hit my stride. My breathing and heartbeat will have adjusted to the rhythm of the movement and all my systems will have produced enough hormones to repeat the task at hand. A typical run for me is about ten to twenty miles depending on the day of the week. A lot of people say running is bad for your joints. Those people are typically overweight or dumb enough to run on concrete or asphalt. Oops. Well, at least I'm not overweight. At about ten miles my body will begin to shiver as it runs low on the chemicals it had initially pumped into the system. This is the signal that it is time to produce more such chemicals. In my typical environment, the atmosphere is conditioned to optimal temperature and humidity for this kind of workout. The room is sixty-eight degrees, with a humidity index of 45 percent. This tunnel feels clammy. It is cold and wet, when I sweat I feel it tearing the strength out of my core, my heat, and I feel my body has to work three times as hard to maintain comfort and homeostasis. The constant ducking and weaving around obstacles changes the rhythm of the steps to an almost unrecognizable break-beat. I feel like I'm moving to dance hall reggae while being chased by an army of tiny clones.

I am able to keep ahead of them, even just barely is a swiftly challenged comfort. I feel the two mile plateau coming as the climb to a regular pace evens out. I squint ahead at the deepening run, perspective points converging into a single dot, parallel lines are an illusion of mathematics to me now. My adrenaline and sympathetic nervous system determine the rules of reality at the moment. My nostrils are flaring in and out in the mildew laden air. Try not to imagine being colonized by tiny black particles with psychic field manipulation. Try not to imagine getting some undiagnosable brain cognitive disorder from this long hole. Try not to think about Hanta virus and anthrax being kicked up by my heels into swirling clouds advancing as surely upon me and as quickly or quicker than the wall of fur and teeth behind me, the turbulent flow of particulate matter in an atmospheric system somehow getting ahead of it's propagating force as if by use of magic. A rooster tail of biological hazard back-drafting down the hallway in a debris trail of meaningless figures tallied and crawled over by the eighteen toed menace which is slower than me, and not by much, and surely can overwhelm my advantages by pure number in an enclosed space.

The two mile feeling has come and gone. I am still running. I don't have to look behind me, the sounds of scampering soft padded feet with sharp claws and the whispering squeaky breathing of trillions of tiny lungs confirms that I have not outrun my assailants. I feel fear in my heart. I feel despair. If I have not been able to outrun these creatures in five miles. What makes me think I can do it in ten or twenty? And what about after that? I've never run more than twenty miles and that usually on a Sunday before brunch and a huge afternoon nap, followed by cocktails upon waking. This is set to be an underground marathon through the shit and piss of a legion of filth, under threat of death by a thousand rabid cuts. All I can do for now is run. I push the other thoughts to the back of my mind where they shout over the walls I build around them, nagging me, pulling my concentration away from the path ahead of me.

I get so overwhelmed by my own doubts and managing inner turmoil that I trip over a broom stick laying across the floor. I don't have the time it takes me to wonder who in fuck's sake has left a broomstick here, here where it is apparent that nobody has done even the slightest amount of upkeep in a number of decades. A broomstick is some sort of irony I can spend days laughing about, if I get out of here, but not now. If I take the energy needed to laugh, combined with the helplessness of a laughing man, I will be covered in fur and chisel shaped bite marks before I can end my hysterics.

The broomstick slides under the impact of the plantar arch of my foot. It bites into the ligaments in that soft spot between my heel and big toe pad. It hurts like a son-of-a-bitch. That pressure point screams up my leg tightening every muscle and tendon I have managed to loosen up in my miles long run, and I fall forward, my leg collapsing beneath me in a shower of pain and expletives as I tumble out the momentum into a cold sprawl in a heap. Boxes of numbers on paper topple and spill over me in a cascade as I flounder and skid up to a ready-set-go again before I'd even come to a stop, hoping to carry some momentum from the tragically comic accident into a second wind. I go forward on a contused ankle and a barking shin. Now my rhythm is hobbled by my own displaced balance as well as the obstacles in my path.

The mice have closed the gap and I feel them sinking their jaws into the rubber of my heels. Feel their skulls popping underfoot as I roll onward, hoping to regain my lead, working out the injuries in motion. Another fall like that and I will be consumed. Now I am struck paranoid about the path ahead. I measure my steps more carefully, it becomes gut-wrenching to step into a darkened space beyond a stack of boxes in the shadow of calculations I have not worked out. I hear the voices of the mice in my head doing trinomials, derivatives, and integration functions in tandem. They are trying to take me down again with their multitudinous thoughts. My brain is bigger than a hundred of theirs, perhaps a thousand, but they are dividing the processing load over a network of trillions, perhaps an infinite number of nodes.

I feel my pace quicken in panic as the shivers at mile ten bring with them unexpected discomfort like having red hot knitting needles inserted beneath my scapulae. If I puke I have to keep running through the heaving of my diaphragm. Is that even possible to puke and run at the same time? The pain makes me sure to find out soon. I feel the warmth rush back into my spine and gut as the spigot of resources within me turns on for its regular scheduled dump of new and intriguing hormones into my system. I throw up into my mouth and spit it, spray it in a ghastly exhale to my left, leaving an explosive mark of bile and not much else upon the wall.

The Mice Will Eat Your Shoes!

A few mice who are crawling along beside me are drenched in barf, which again, might be something I can laugh about someday. But not now as I career along and those few hapless targets of my projectile vomit find themselves blown flat against the concrete wall of the tunnel. They drop off in disgust at what has happened to them, for even to a mouse this seems an affront to decency. They are quickly overcome by their brethren who, unable to smell the mousiness of their mates, eat them alive. A mini-bloodbath scene in my wake as two or three mice are rendered into a snack for two or three hundred more who find my bile enticing or delicious, or just alien enough to warrant annihilation. The terrified squeals of those two or three lost in sacrifice are not audible above the din of the remainder. They are infinitesimal.

In the winking lights of the overhead bulbs I see something change in my pinpoint horizon. As I continue to converge in fractal intimacy with what appears at last to be the end of the tunnel I feel a push to give myself enough time to breach whatever barrier lays in wait. I change my stride from a loping long distance gait to a sprint, kicking my heels all the way up to my anus and burning through the last of my reserves to close the last quarter mile or so in about sixty seconds, which is extremely fast for a sixty something year old white dude considering there aren't any brunch lines around here.

At the end of the tunnel, I do not look behind me. I come slamming up against a solid door. I feel the knob.

Lemons: In an Orchard

It turns. I push, nothing. I pull, it comes toward me as the fastest of the mice begin to crawl up the backs of my pants. I swing around and inside and shut the door hard on the spines of several gutsy fur-balls, their livers and spleens and hearts and eyeballs channeling themselves into some kind of jewel encrusted slime upon the jamb. The door stands strong as a million tiny bodies press up against it. I look around the room and am stupefied to realize I am not alone.

The mice didn't eat your shoes, did they? he says, looking through his kaleidoscope at me, or the door, or some fucking astral projection in his imagination.

They sure as fuck tried, I say, inspecting the filthy soles of my runners. The concrete and basement mildew spores swirling about them have created turbulent patterns of black dust and the once white spongy rubber are now a filthy gray. There are grass stains on my toes, presumably from being dragged out of a river and laid out to dry like primitive laundry. There are bloody splats where I've crushed mice to death.

That door won't hold them forever, he says casually.

What the fuck do you mean, I say? Are you fucking kidding me right now? Mice are gonna knock down that steel door that I ran into full speed and almost broke my wrists on?

Yes, something like that, he says. Let me read your cards.

Let you what? Read my what the fuck?

Your. Cards. He is unusually lucid and assertive. I note that he wears a crown today, and that it is squirming, no swarming about his skull. Bits of it crawl over his cheeks while he speaks, their little hips covered in lemon pollen.

Fuck me.

I don't think so, he says, and holds out a deck. Choose.

H-h-how many? I can't believe I am participating and feel it is certainly under duress.

Your choice, he says.

I reach out, a small bee alights upon the top of my thumb and cautions me, choose well. He departs leaving a blessing in the form of a yellowish orange smudge. I grab the whole deck and pull a fistful of cards from the center, handing them to the beekeeper. He looks delighted. Here's the rest of them too, I say and hand him the rest.

Hmm, seven hearts, deuce spades, king diamonds. He pulls out a banker's box full of papers, lifts a folder from the top of the stack within, withdraws the topmost sheet of printed figures and scrawls in ink a few more digits.

At this, the sound of tiny bodies hurtling against the door ceases. A small river of blood creeps under the door. Dust settles from the lintel above. A swaying light bulb over the beekeeper's head is stilled by a long fingered hand reaching up without looking, grasping the hot bulb. He holds it for a few seconds then releases his fingers, red from contact, and the bulb stays put. He puts my cards back into the deck and shuffles them absent-mindedly.

Aren't you going to tell me what it means? I ask.

It's not for you to know, he says, besides, you don't believe in this crap.

It's hard to maintain my skepticism around you, I say.

The mice will not be eating your shoes today. Would you like a sandwich? At this he sniggers.

No, I say. I think I've had enough of your sandwiches. Can you tell me how to get back to the grove?

I can.

Will you please tell me how to get back to the grove?

I will.

I swear I almost punch him. Then please do it, I say between gritted teeth.

He turns and looks behind him. There is a red velvet curtain. It brings back nightmare shadows from the movie theater. I go to it and draw it aside. There is an elevator door. I press the call button. Such Sweet Thunder starts playing. Duke Ellington brings a classy vibe to this otherwise miasmatic pit. I almost find myself tapping my foot, but feel the amused eyes of the beekeeper upon me and don't want to lend him any more satisfaction at my own expense.

The elevator car comes, creaking and popping. The brakes engage near the bottom and it rides a school full of fingernails down chalkboards to a thudding landing. The silence which precedes the parting of the doors is final. I look back at the beekeeper and step inside. The gates close, then the outer doors, he doesn't look up, just waves one spindly old hand over his shoulder at me, goodbye.

As I should have expected by now, the walls of the box are lined with numbered buttons, all out of order, some far longer than could reasonably be connected with anyplace in vertical space, unless we are going to the moon, or Mars, or Pluto. They are colorful, aged by time into hues all tinged with the golden amber of fossilized Bakelite plastic. I look around for something useful. In the midst of my beginning to make sense of things, the box starts climbing on it's own.

Rather than risk altering an unknown and possibly default position, I just back away from the walls and stand at the center of the lift, waiting to see where it has decided to take me. The numbers flash from floor to ceiling as I traverse the levels of these catacombs.

My anxiety is quelled by the absence of pursuers. I am not in a hurry after my run through the tunnel. This thing could basically take me just about anywhere that wasn't the bottom of a hell-scape administrators nightmare and I will be fine. The door could open upon a besieged children's show backstage, with actors running around faceless in furry inspired bodysuits carrying trays of human entrails and I'd probably walk out amidst that carnival and start searching for a tray of Dom, ready to take a seat amongst the most flagrantly unbelonging clowns as long as there were no sign of rodentia among them. I might permit a rabbit suit, but if chuck e. cheese shows up, I would probably use a chicken satay to dig his fucking heart out.

The lift goes on and on. I have no concept of space or time left, as I am not exerting myself and can't see beyond the buttons blinking in and out of sequence in front of me. I begin watching them for a pattern, but none can be established. If there is a pattern it is too big for me to register within my limited memory. I could be in this lift for a decade without knowing if it weren't for my sense of thirst which has been growing since last night outside the cave. I have not found any water, nor did I have the time to think about it when I was being run down by the vermin army, but now that my mind is wandering, it is filled with images from the dream of water and waves. I find myself greedily drinking from my own subconscious. My sense of hunger is awakened too. I wonder what time it will be when I return, if I return to the village. Will I be able to find something other than a watering can at whatever hour it will be?

I reach in my pocket and pull out my shattered watch and the pendant on a snapped chain. The movement slips out of the casing and between my fingers. The kinetic pendulum separates from its post and skitters like a bug across the floor of the box and out under the door. I look at the pendant draped over my knuckles. Prising it open reveals the pictures inside once again. The older woman in the photo now looks very familiar to me. I bend forward to attempt to retrieve bits of my watch from the floor when the bell chimes and the doors open.

14— I SEE A PORTAL OPEN

I look up, at the office in front of me.

My office.

Secretaries, admins and paralegals all look at me from the corners of their eyes, not willing to appear so distractible as to turn and make eye contact. If I want something from one of them, I'll walk right up and interrupt them. They know I am here and their entire gestalt subconscious sphincter tightens despite my own uncharacteristic surprise at having arrived at the office from a subterranean maze some fifty years in the sideways future. I look down at my clothes and hands. That's more like it. A dark gray suit, crisp linen white shirt, red tie with some little grid of repeating designs on it. My cologne is substantial, but not overbearing. My shoes, oh they feel so good, my cognac crocodile shoes. My feet are inside velvet cushions.

Nervously, I step from the box, my peripheral vision inspecting the crack between carriage and shaft as I cross that razor thin crevasse. I expect it to be glowing red hot with center of the earth madness. It is dark and empty and has completely swallowed up the movement of my watch. I look at my wrist. I am wearing my gold Movado, casing intact, ticking away as it always does. I shake my wrist near my ear and someone says, still ticking? as they pass with a folder full of papers.

I say, hold on a minute. Let me see that folder, please. Jenny stops cold in her tracks, turns and hands the folder to me without so much as an equivocating eye movement. I eye her with suspicion as I take the folder and open it. Merrick and Williams manufacturing plant consolidated yearly reports for years 2010-2020. Blah blah blah. I hand it back to her, choking back the calamity in my head that tells me I will find folders composed of that one single endless numeral, calculating itself on into infinity. Thanks Jenny, I say.

Does that look like what you wanted me to send over? she asks.

Lemons: In an Orchard

Oh, yes, that's perfect, I say, having no idea what she is talking about. I am in this world, my world, and none of it feels familiar anymore. I feel like an alien in my own life. There is this slick brick in my lower inside jacket pocket. I pull it out and stare at the glass screen in front of me. It recognizes me and unlocks. Several notifications materialize describing to me what I am apt to be doing today. There is no room for serendipity. Jenny turns with efficacious energy to bear her package onward to wherever I have asked her to bring it.

I search for my office along the outside ring of rooms around the cubicles. Every one I go to is occupied. I just keep walking, peeking surreptitiously into the rooms looking for my name on a desk somewhere. I reach the end of the row, unmolested. There is another elevator. The sign says Executive Suites. That sounds like me. I press the call button and the door opens. I ride the elevator up and get off a floor or two above. The timbre of the space is entirely different. There is no clutter whatsoever. I know this is me. My comfort in emptiness proclaims itself. I feel the pull to the biggest office, the one with all the windows and light. I walk up and enter, find it empty. My name is on the door. I sit in the big leather swivel chair. Feel it electronically mold to my form and massage my legs with infrared heat.

The phone on the desk is a dinosaur with dumb lights and buttons, many of them flashing. I pull my mobile out again and look through the messages. Lisa has texted. She is interested to know what my plans are for dinner tonight, should she grab something? I press the call button. My hand pauses a moment as I stare into space before lifting the phone to my ear with a tic and a grimace as I feel that my sense of reality might be slipping.

It rings seven times and goes to voicemail.

She texts again, is everything alright?

I answer, yes, I just wanted to hear your voice.

That's weird.

I've had an interesting day. I wanted to talk about it.

Do you want me to call you when I finish what I'm working on?

No, that's okay.

What about dinner? she texts and I put down the phone, unsure how to answer such a question. If I have been restored to my fortunate life, it must mean something for the things I have seen, been shown. Chet living out his life in the little village really seemed to have given him some vivacity and life of his own. If the world was going to end, did we not need to be in that grove? All of us.

This life I have built is an empty shell. It is leukemia. I look at my desk again. Empty. I open the drawers, empty. I look around the office. Clean. There is no warmth. I feel a chill. Perhaps it has always been that way and I just became aware of it. This alienation is the system I have developed around my conscious entity. My skeleton dances inside me. I look for something to throw. There is a laptop computer, shut, its power cord neatly rolled and stored in a drawer, the back of the folded screen is freshly wiped with an anti static cloth. I pick it up. My face pulls to one side and teeth are visible. The computer held in my hands pulls itself up high and then to the ground in an anticlimactic slap. Nothing even falls out. There are no sparks or explosions. The laptop smacks the ground and its functionality disintegrates leaving the casing intact. I throw it at the wall and it disappears into a slot shaped hole in the cream colored drywall.

A voice from the office next door shouts, what the fuck? It's Timmons. He comes rushing around to my door. What the fuck was that? he says again.

What? I ask.

The fucking laptop that just came through our partition wall is what. What the fuck, man? There's fucking debris all over my office. Have you fucking lost it? He is shaking, angry, but also scared. He is no match for me physically and I assume he must be contemplating the possibility that I have had a psychotic break and am about to pummel him into a mush. He has his cell phone in his hand.

I look past him into the large open central executive lounge area. There are several others who've come out to see what the fuck is going on in my office. There is a variety-show of emotions on their faces. Some of them wrinkle their foreheads, others bare their teeth, some hold their hands up over their faces. Roberts with his jacket slung over his arm and his attache gripped firmly in his hand strides for the elevator and leaves.

Timmons backs out of my office. I've said nothing, offered no explanation, which could only mean I am stifling another explosion. He goes back to his office. I can hear him calling human resources. The others kind of mill about in a pool of anxiety.

Billy says, We 're still on for squash this afternoon?

I look at him like he were a talking dog. He just averts his eyes and slinks away. Nothing he wants to face at the moment. A bomb has gone off. I am that bomb. Whatever has happened to me is beyond their comprehension. I know that. It doesn't stop me from hating them now, for being the ethically vacant bunch that we all are. My shift in personality is the flickering light bulb revealing the lemon juice invisible ink of our secret biographies. Everyone is very uncomfortable.

I open my center drawer. I look into the empty wooden box. Fuck. Give me a folder, I yell. Billy, a junior exec, eager to please, brings me the incidentals on Grover McNiland Corp. I ball up each page of that hundred page document while he watches silently. Then I pull the Zippo out of my pocket. The scent of lemon oil cleanses the air of the room. Billy's face drops as he realizes he is party to arson.

I walk to the elevator while all these assholes scramble to find the working fire extinguisher. The alarms are going off. With my back to the doors I shout into the executive lounge, mice will eat your shoes! I get inside the box and press the button for the lower level. Walking out amongst the calm bovine faces of the herd below, I see Jenny again. I say, Jenny, I quit. Her face tells me she doesn't know how to react. If it's a joke, should she laugh? If it's not, should she try and stop me?

The elevator I arrived on looks normal again. It brings me to the ground floor where I find my Jeep in my parking spot. I start the engine and drive. Buildings shrink as the trail leads out from the city, east into the rolling fields in the vast valleys between the Rockies and the hills of Malibu. The dirt gets richer. The sun is invisible.

❋ ❋ ❋

Bakersfield is an eyesore full of mechanical plungers fucking the dirt for oil. These industrial dinosaurs like so many drinking birds level their hollow gaze to the horizon which fails to approach. Sterile lifeless forms routing out the space of their days. I turn North and the poison oil fields give way to the agriculture of robot run farms. Drones everywhere carrying fruits of all shapes and colors. I drive until I see the yellow gems hanging in the branches above me. Then I pull over and get out of the car.

I am hot so I leave my jacket. My pants are itching me. All I have for an alternative are a pair of jogging pants and a t-shirt. I put them on. I text Lisa and Chet and tell them where to find me. Then I put the phone in the glove-box and leave it on so it can be geo-located. My hands are sweating. My vision shaking. My ears feel cold. I trudge into the lemon grove, one last time. No food, no water, though I know how to siphon off the robot irrigation until I find my way through the portal. That doorway that I have never seen worries me. Finding it, and my way back to the village, is the only release for this fettered soul.

In the village the drums are pounding. Dancers whirl around and through each other. One big family of barefoot farmers tending crops in a world gone by. The women with their hair all bleached by citrus juice and sunshine, their skin darkened by the same catalyst, hold up the entire village under the matriarchal authority of Abuela. There is a sense, I worry that I have simply been used, and that use drove me mad. Some out of this world power like I never thought reasonable has come over me. In it's corona, I have felt the utter uselessness of everything I have done to preserve what I thought were my values, and the destructiveness of those values to my family is in stark relief to the unity that will form in my absence.

The torches pound up and down to the beat of the coyote skin drums. The resonating lemon wood barrels give a sweet and sour rejoinder to the feet stepping lively around each other. I feel a toe slide under my heel and it escapes being crushed by milliseconds as I clumsily falter backward. Or forward, through time to a place that left me behind, for good reason, though I suspect by accident. No one person could possibly control all these portals and slippages. No great plan could be using me in a tiny little village at the end of the human journey. My power has always been in the clever use of the system I was born into. My madness comes from seeing that system dismantled and tossed aside, either by choice or consequence.

Visions from the cave world below the grove come back to me. Were those sons of bitches following me right now? Is my family coming to join me? I look for signs of inter-world transport. I don't know if it was a shimmer, or a wave, or some magic combination of actions, a pile of coyote entrails arranged like a Basqiuat painting. I look for anything that isn't orderly. I look for any sign of declension from the pattern which symbolizes infinite reproduction and robotic algorithm. I look for old men with sandwiches. I run through the whipping lower branches. They tear at my skin. The feeling of transgression is ecstatic. Where are you? I shout aloud into the thicket of suns beneath the smoldering clouds from burning mountains. Take me back! I shout into the dense curated wilderness, hoping that some breach will hear me. Some chasm between worlds open up and admit me to the place where I am penniless and where in the absence of power, I feel peace. Then I see a honeybee.

She looks drunk. She's been breathing smoke all day and her flight dances from flowerless branch to late yellow ball and back. The ground is a wasteland of dirt, not a clover or dandelion in sight. No soft blades of grass for her to tumble down into and cool off. I follow her, my path becoming hers. My legs scattering beneath my careening torso. I become the drunk by proxy of my motion. The movements work in reverse to stimulate my nervous system into reeling. She flies and I follow, off course from the row, the easy path. She goes right between two tall trees which are pressed tightly together and I drop to my hands and knees and crawl along behind her, craning my neck and twisting my head sideways to keep an eye on her flight. The sound of her wings is a transformer, an electric current sweeping along a microphone. It is a lonely sound. She moves quickly as though she knows I am chasing her.

Looking up to keep my eye on the honeybee, I see into the ash gray vault above me. The great emptiness draws my breath and my chest hurts a little. Across the firmament, traversing a wasteland in search of rabbits, flies a hawk. Its motion from left to right in my field of view. It must be a sign. I run willy-nilly along behind the honeybee without looking where I am going. She must be going somewhere. Out of this hot smoke air comes another buzzing sound. It swoops in and grapples her in mid air. A wasp, twice her size, bloodthirsty and strange, picks her out of her drunken ranging and carries her off, paralyzed in its carnivorous grasp.

Lemons: In an Orchard

I stand stupid there. What the fuck am I doing? Maybe I should just go back and spend some money. I am a frugal man, but perhaps that's what I need to escape this trap. Spend a little freely the money I know will never run out in three lifetimes. While I ponder, another sound creeps in. It is not a river, but it is in a sense a current. It is a much bigger buzzing. I listen carefully and follow my ears. The sound grows louder, angrier, ravenous. I know what it is before I find it.

Pushing aside the branches and ducking under the thickest of them, I lean forward into the smell of a rotting carcass. Dog's blood fills my nose. Dried into the soil, it crushes under my fingertips and floats as a cloud to cover my face. I see a thousand wasps on the body of a dead coyote. It is dead, but it is squirming with life. Its insides pulse with the breath of maggots. Its fur bristles with the antagonism of a crawling army of mechanical killers. They pinch and lick the rotting flesh and are driven into a state of murderous climax by the cold corpse. Here is the birth of life.

I crawl in further under the tree. Hornets fly in front of my face. They angrily buzz in my ears. I feel them landing on my back through the t-shirt as thudding lumps of crash-landed DaVinci flying machines. Feel them picking their way along the white cotton, their prickly feet searching for the edge of the fabric to crawl beneath, as I crawl along the ground. I feel the first one reach the nape of my neck and wonder how committed they are to this assault. A searing pain as it stabs me.

I See a Portal Open

My hand goes up in reflexive shock and smashes the bug against my skin. This explosion of pheromones undetectable to me is like a clarion call to the mass of insects and they begin to leave the dog, jaws full of pincered off hunks of putrid flesh and they come for me. I close my eyes and fling myself upon the corpse. Covered in a thousand stinging biting crystallized objects of fury, I pull open the bowels of that lowly creature and dig my hands inside. I can feel the wriggling of intestines full of meal worms and larvae of insects. I feel the life of this object appearing dead before me.

With my eyes closed I see the portal open. I hear the drums. I see the dancers again. I taste their whisky and feel the warmth of that sun. I smell the pungent and meaty white flowers blooming everywhere. I hear Katrina, sitting naked on my lap whispering something in Spanish into my ear. The river behind me washes its eternal current of stories along in a fluid embrace of truth which changes, not from day to day, but moment to moment, each one as inseparable from the whole as life from life.

The End

ABOUT THE AUTHOR

David John Baer McNicholas is a wizard who lives in a spray painted Thor El Dorado shuttle bus. He is on his third regeneration and is a professional ghost hunter. He loves animals. His pets are the spirits of two deceased Bettas. Frank and Scott Baio. They haunt the radio and the engine respectively.

BOOKS BY THIS AUTHOR

L.I.E.S.

An alt-novel in the form of a lit-rag. Boris and Aliane are untethered from a common reality while they seek out their identities.

Hosted by ghostofamerica.net   Read for free there.

Callously Wanton

The anarcho-journal of a young Hot Wheels Spaulding struggling to find love and meaning.

Hosted by ghostofamerica.net   Read for free there.

The 9x9 of Love and Other Stories

A narrator in a time dilated bubble. An android love interest. Similar messy things.   Out of print.

Made in the USA
Middletown, DE
26 September 2023

39295716R00135